OCTOBER'S HARVEST

By
Charity Williams

October's Harvest

Copyright © 2020 by Charity Williams

Cover Photography from canva.com

ISBN: 9798631448483

To all the black girls who don't believe they can be horror writers.
You can. Now write.

FALL

CHAPTER 1

My name was October Harbuck, and I lived in a cult. Although me and my brother weren't born there, our destinies had been intertwined with the farm since its conception.

The place where we lived was named Blue Corn. The Blue Corn Farm to outsiders. The farm was our whole world. We lived and died in Blue Corn. It was a place where no one came and no one left. It was a place built a long time ago by a man named William Walsh and generation after generation of his family controlled the place with an iron grip. It was William Walsh who was instructed by God to trap us here.

I always imagined how this place got started. What would've led the founding prophet William Walsh to learn the liquid gold language that he would use against us. His suit must've served him well as he traveled over mountains and ridges to get to the farm's flat piece of land, and the good book must've given him a sense of purpose as his boat swam over the passage to the new world. Whether this was where the divine revelation from God took place no one will ever know.

The land that the community was built on had once belonged to the woods where the earth was brittle and the soil as dry as the air. Sometimes in the spring the pond that lay in the thicket of trees returned. In the winter it froze over. By the hands of William Walsh, the land was replenished. Growing grass. Bountiful fields of corn. The fruit of William Walsh's labor blossomed, and it bloomed into the place where our entire lives were conceived. It was supposed to leave us wanting less, but the blossoming fields only left me wanting more.

***

"October?"

I snapped my head over from the window to look over at the class, but everyone was looking at the teacher, Sister Jennifer. She was William Walsh's great-great-granddaughter and our current prophet's sister. She hit the chalkboard with her stick, and I flinched. I placed my hands flat on the desk in a manner of respect and discipline.

Our schoolhouse was small. The older kids like me had class in the afternoon where we learned how to read and write and basic arithmetic like adding and subtracting. The smaller kids like my brother had class in the morning. I was seventeen. This was my last year in school before I would be assigned, and since I was a Sinner, I would be assigned a job that would be equal punishment.

My family wasn't always Sinners. They were Saints, and they got to live in the big houses with running water and food filled fridges. My brother and I made them Sinners, and after last year, our place in the poor part of the community was sealed forever. Sinners got leaky ceilings in their cottages and stale bread for dinner. While Saints worked in the community, Sinners worked in the cornfields, the mill, and the rest of the farm. Smoke from the mill cast a grayish shadow over the skies, and after the workers got off from work, they scattered out of the building with sunken faces. My father used to complain about his aching back and cramped fingers. My mother suffered from cracked nails and calloused palms.

My father, who loved his job at the mill, was a man known by all, befriended by a few. But he had an extraordinary amount of influence on anyone who disregarded their best instincts and associated with him. He was a hard worker and was bound to his job just like everyone else was. In fact, he would have been supervising, he had the charisma. He would have been the head of the mill. He had the brains, but as he was returning home from work, he vanished. Disappeared off the face of the earth.

Though the news of his disappearance was talked about all over the community, soon it had to be forgotten. The rumor had said that he left the community. That somehow he was able to climb the tall wooden fence that bordered Blue Corn until he made his great escape into the great unknown. But that wasn't the truth.

The disappearance left a grieving wife in Blue Corn: my mother. She stopped smiling for some time. She didn't speak for a while. She said that she could hear his calls in the wind, and that she could taste him in everything that she ate, that she couldn't stand the sight of anything. It reminded her so much of him. At times, I think that included us. Her love no longer reached her eyes which had turned gray and hard as steel. A dark shadow lived on her face feeding off of her grief.

After my father's disappearance, my little brother was more aware of our mother's presence. Brayley had turned twelve that summer and I had turned seventeen. When our mother went to cook, he would steady himself beside her, with his hands out to help. I would talk endlessly to fill in the rest of the space. After a while, the radio would turn on, and Josef's announcements drifted through the house. I was an expert at ignoring things, but even his voice would find a way to pour into my ear.

When dinner came, I would help set the table, and then we would sit around the table and eat together. But we were always watching her. She was our queen whether she wanted us to worship her or not. We bowed to her because we were afraid that she would vanish like our father.

When the last remnants of summer fell away, my mother decided that love would never find her again and soon felt it a thing of longing just like the summer nights. That was when love appeared on the doorstep in the form of our current prophet, Josef Walsh, William Walsh's great-great grandson.

His plan had been to stay for dinner to tell us the good news. My mother was going to be remarried. Josef explained to us that God made my mother for a reason, and it was to be married to someone who would take care of her the right way. Then Josef went on to say that my father was never the right man, but there was someone out there who was the right one for her. I soon found myself ignoring what he said but watching him. His eyes searched hungrily over my mother's face like he was looking for something. Some kind of reaction that she was happy, but my mother hadn't given him the courtesy. Josef was a man who could make an unbeliever a believer. A man who knew how to use his charm in a way that made him dangerous. After all, the most beautiful roses have thorns.

I cried that night, a small cry that didn't wake Brayley as he slept beside me nor wake my mother who slept in the bedroom beside ours. The sound would pause briefly and then I would think. I knew that Josef wanted my mother for himself. He was going to make my mother his wife. He had always wanted us out of the way.

A month later and I still mourned, because in the autumn season it had never occurred to me that my mother was going to be married to the prophet, the dashing Josef Walsh who wore nice clothes and combed hair, and who remembered the name of every person in the community, and who preached his fire and brimstone and who smiled even when no one else did, with an impersonal manner that we all resented because no one actually liked him.

Josef was the bringer of death. The dead look of the community stirred a strange enthusiasm in him, and made him forgetful of the real reason his great-great grandfather started this place. He would look at each of us with the most loveliest expression, and then close us up in the palms of his hands since he did own us. This was death. But all the same, it was how he loved us best.

***

Soon the autumn fog covered the afternoon air lightly like a hot breath on glass. The children finally came, running out for recess. The boys wrestled each other, landing in dirt and pulling dust up into the air, and the girls hung around the swings and talked and watched the boys. This happened every day, a familiar wonder. The sun would rise, and I would daydream about what lay beyond the fence that stretched from Blue Corn on every side. And I would feel lonely. It was the same kind of loneliness that my brother felt as I watched him as he seemed to belong to a world all of his own. Dark skin was all we had known, first the outrage and then the dirty looks, and now most people did not wish to acknowledge us.

Now, to comfort myself, I waved at him. My brother noticed me. His face was delicate yet solemn just as it was when he was a baby. Brayley would watch my face with a different intensity than when he watched my mother. He didn't want me to take on the postures and dialects of our community, to assimilate my life into theirs, so that they would never feel invaded upon. My love for Brayley was immaculate, my attitude towards him loving. He saw me not as other people were because I had never taught him to be like them. I wanted him to be himself.

Nikki, my best friend, glanced over at me. She had freckled skin and red hair. She was pretty in an unconventional way, but others managed to make her feel like she wasn't. She sat in the desk beside me, and her eyebrows rose, warning me of Sister Jennifer. Through all of my complaints, Nikki's eyes were always wide with excitement to learn. She was eager to drink from the fountain of knowledge. I sighed and moved my attention to the chalkboard in an attempt to pay attention to Sister Jennifer's lesson.

Nikki loved me and my family. She had three other siblings and parents, who sometimes had to sacrifice their own plates to feed their children, their throats parched, hunger pulsing in their temples. In our decade long friendship, Nikki confided in me as I confided in her.

When Nikki learned of my father's disappearance, she began to urge me to be careful. She believed something wasn't right with his disappearance. I pretended to believe her in an attempt to appease her. In this small place, no one could leave without someone noticing and no one could just disappear in a place that was as tightly controlled as we were. She proved to be right.

***

"So has your mother decided yet?"

"What choice does she have? She either marries him or-"

"Marries him."

We sat at one of the picnic tables in the corner of the school's backyard, food in front of us. We were not inclined to eat. I could hear the voices of the other students carry over to us. Students, who were fond of grayish mush and raw carrot sticks, gathered to chat, while we picked over our food. We would be looked at by others who would judge, stare, and watch us, charged with keeping us near them but not too close.

"You're going to have to call him Father, you know?"

"I will…as soon as hell freezes over."

"You shouldn't curse," Nikki said.

"Should you really be eating that carrot?"

It was them. As in Genevieve Walsh, Cora Davidson, and Raven Collier. They were everyone's enemy yet people still wanted to be like them. They sat in front of us smiling incapable of pure emotion. They were privileged. They were deemed as Saints. People that Josef believed were touched by God and untouched by us. Genevieve was in charge because she was Josef's niece. It was said that when the bells rang the girls would step down the stairs in unison and they would sing, and others would sing back to them, their voice and their followers' voice, on and on, between harmony and murderous symphony. After a while Genevieve's dark eyes would bore into your soul as Raven whistled along, and Cora flirted with her blonde hair. The song of the siren, and no doubt their spell would be cast.

I sighed. "Leave us be Genevieve."

"Or what? You're gonna call your father the vanishing king," she spoke with venom. Her words were sharp. In my head, I called her a corneater. The kind that slithered between the stalks looking to bite the ones whose hunger got the best of them. "Your 'mother' better take my uncle's offer or she's in for a rude awakening."

Genevieve could wave it all away with her hand and waved she did. I shuddered, she winked, and went back to pretending as if nothing had happened.

I glanced at Nikki, and she shrugged. It was a mystery to her too. Mystery plagued itself over Blue Corn into its people. Even into the boy whose very existence was a constant reminder of things I would never have.

Ever since I could remember I have had a crush on Drew Keegan. He carried himself like a dreamer. Or maybe he was still mourning as well. Before my family became the brunt of conversation, his family held the title. His mother had died a little before my father had disappeared. Drew's green eyes and golden hair and olive skin always made me fear that he would never notice me. And I couldn't stop thinking about him. I was certain that he would never accept me.

"You should be careful," Nikki said.

"About what?"

Nikki followed my gaze to Drew who sat at the table across from us. "I can see it in your eyes. It's no secret that you like him, but Cleansing is coming soon and then you'll stop thinking about him for a while."

Nikki was not a girl of excess, and so her crush, as it became more and more ironic, was surprising. It was Zan Hutchinson who was still brisk and bright when most of us had sunk into the ordinary cycle of every day. He had bright eyes and a messy haze of dark hair. He had submitted to this life in a way that was both terrifying but overwhelmingly suspicious. A smile was always plastered on his face from ear to ear. When he walked the halls, eyes lowered and knees bowed. Sometimes he laughed when he saw us or washed his hands. In my fondest memory of Zan, I remember him accidentally dumping a tray over our heads. Even then he was still good looking.

"Do you remember what Zan did to us?" I would ask, but Nikki would always look away.

A long moment of quiet fell upon us. We ate our mush, choking it down with our small drink of water. The taste was awful, but it filled our stomachs.

"I don't believe he ran away."

"Me neither, but it's probably best if we just go with it."

"Why?" I asked her.

Nikki looked up from her plate. Her face was grimly set, and her blue eyes darkened with an intensity that frightened me. "People who find answers disappear like your father."

CHAPTER 2

School felt like an eternity and only when the bell rang were we allowed out of our seats and to go about our day. Like always Genevieve and the other Saints lagged behind. At the sound of the bell, they didn't feel the need to rush out of their seats, like we did. Saints were exempt from working in the cornfields. I watched as Drew was suddenly surrounded by everyone. Everyone hoping to get the chance to talk to the community's golden boy.

"Off you go," Sister Jennifer said, shooing us Sinners out of the schoolhouse. It was time for us to work. The corn wasn't going to pick itself.

On our way to the cornfields, we were met by Brayley and Nikki's little sister, Nadia. Nadia's red ponytail swayed from side to side as she and Brayley whispered to each other. I listened because something was wrong. I could tell by the way Nadia looked at

Brayley with a look of sadness and love. Nadia was to Brayley what Drew should have been to me, but somehow Nadia was more possible for him.

"You okay?"

"I'm fine."

"You're not."

"Garrett's a jerk."

"He's a Saint."

"It doesn't matter."

I couldn't listen anymore. I knew something had happened. A fight. Between him and the boy who always would be there to remind us who we were. He was the worst of Blue Corn.

Nadia's hand brushed against Brayley. I glanced at Nikki who was staring at them. She had a small smile on her face. Brayley and Nadia's relationship was like ours sometimes. How we were connected by nothing other than familiarity but we had each other. Unlike Nikki and I, Brayley and Nadia's relationship was ridiculed and they were always threatened.

We walked through the thick atmosphere. Sometimes the sun would be out. Today it wasn't. Above I watched the clouds as they drifted by. Even though the fog from earlier had disappeared, it was still gray and there was a stillness in the air.

We finally arrived at the cornfields which were the trademark of the farm. I looked over at the green stalks. In the fall, their color was lush. Green as the grass underneath them. The yellow peeked out ready to be picked.

For some reason the cornfields were a source of pleasure for the Blue Corn Farm. It was producing and everlasting. Several acres of it grew. The people here always looked to expand it, until the tall stalks reached high into the heavens. Farmers heaped piles of corn into buckets that were sent out across the whole community and to the outside world. We ate corn almost every night. Cream corn. Regular corn. Corn salad. Corn pudding. There were barrels of it. It was how we made our living to be so isolated. It was how we stayed alive.

Some kids were already picking the corn. Some would say the sins of the father shouldn't be passed to the child, but here it was different. Kids were deemed sinners because of their parents' mistakes. For us, it was different. My brother and I were deemed sinners because of who we were. I stared at some of the kids picking the corn. There were some older than me and even younger than Brayley. Some kids had bags underneath their eyes. Some kids had smiles. Pain in their fingers.

I held my palm out as my father would clean my wounds with alcohol.

"I'm sorry pumpkin,"He would say to me as he tended to my wounds. Picking corn was hell on an eight year old's hands. I had about as many blisters and calluses as he did.

"It's okay," I would say to him. He looked up at me. His blue eyes were sharp. Never dull. He never rested in this place.

"It's not okay. It's never okay," he would say. He bowed his head and sighed. "Children shouldn't be put to work. It's not right."

"Well, what are we going to do?" I would ask.

He looked back up at me. "There's always something we can do."

I turned my back to the cornfields.

"Go home," I said to Brayley.

Nikki snapped her head in my direction.

"Why?" he asked. "We can't do that."

Brayley was right. From the moment we were able to go to school, we were expected to spend our afternoons in the cornfields. We all had to contribute in some way.

"You're too young," I said to him. I turned my attention to Nadia. "You too. You should go home."

Nadia looked over at Nikki. Nikki pursed her lips together. Even though she would never agree with me, she didn't want to admit when I was right. "We're supposed to work."

"I want you to go home. Say you're sick. I don't care. Stay home."

"I'll get in trouble," he said to me.

"You won't," I said to him. I looked over my shoulder to see the overseer for the day walking through the rows. If he saw us, Brayley wouldn't be able to get away. "Go. Now."

Nadia grabbed Brayley's hand. She nodded and feigned a smile in Nikki's direction. Nikki nodded in agreement.

I watched as they walked off. Slow at first, but then they picked up the pace and they were running. Far from the fields. I looked over my shoulder again to see that the overseer was coming closer. I turned to go back, but Nikki grabbed my arm.

"They're going to know," Nikki whispered. The overseer had spotted us, and it looked like he was coming our way.

"They can't keep doing this," I said to her. "Starving us and expecting us to break our back to work. It's not okay."

Nikki opened her mouth to say something just as the overseer walked up to us. It was Brother Jack. I remember he worked with my father at the mill. He peered at us from over his glasses.

"You two ladies, okay?" he asked.

"Yes, Brother Jack," we said in unison.

He nodded. "It's good to see you, October."

I nodded and walked past him heading into the cornfields.

Nikki and I found an empty spot to work in. Far enough not to be heard over the stalks and not too far to get from the sight of Brother Jack.

"Bucket," she said, signaling that it was my turn to go get the bucket from him.

I walked to the front of the corn stalks and spotted Brother Jack. I couldn't tell if he was looking directly at me, but I could feel eyes on me. Everyone was always watching me. I picked up the red bucket and looked back at him. He had turned his head, but I knew he was studying me. I walked back to the stalks with the feeling that it was something he had wanted to say.

Nikki and I picked quietly for a while. Our bucket filled as fast as our fingers worked. The stalks were quiet. No one had anything to talk about. We could all sense the fence which was the closest when we were in the fields.

The fence hovered over all of our minds in Blue Corn. When the air glowed in the spring, the exhale of fresh flowers. The wind blew and the smell of freedom. When the ground was wet from summer rain, the rush of excitement at the thought of a slippery escape. In the winter when the air was cold, my fingers twitched and my heart ached. The breath of imagination as I thought about what it would be like to take the climb.

"Why did you do that?" Nikki asked all of a sudden. "It was a risk."

"It's a risk I'm willing to take," I said to her. "Kids shouldn't have to work in the cornfields."

"We shouldn't have to do a lot of things. It's just our way."

"Their way," I corrected her. "And it's the wrong way."

"What do you want us to do, October? Leave? You know that's not happening," Nikki said.

I pulled my hand from out of the stalks as my finger began to sting. I must have scraped it. A tiny cut on my pointer finger began to bleed. I placed my finger in my mouth and began to suck on the wound. A metallic taste filled my mouth.

"Times up!" we could hear Brother Jack yell across the stalks.

Nikki and I each grabbed a handle to the bucket. We were careful not to spill it as we walked to the front of the stalks where the rest of the kids were. Brother Jack was inspecting each of our buckets to make sure that we had our buckets filled. There was supposed to be twenty-five buckets filled every afternoon. Not a drop less.

Nikki nudged me as Brother Jack paused at the bucket beside us. It belonged to a couple of twelve year old girls. One of them coughed into her hands as the other stared down at the ground. She was visibly shaking. The belt in Jack's hand was enough to cause all of us to shake.

"We're sorry Brother Jack. Hannah isn't feeling well and I couldn't do it all by myself," said the girl with the shakes. Her name was Lily.

Brother Jack stepped closer to the girls. I held my breath as we all waited.

"Well..." he started. "I guess Hannah needs to get better then. We'll do better next time."

My jaw dropped. For a second, his eyes drifted over to me. I looked back down and heaved a sigh of relief.

Sometimes the cornfields were our hells. Beautifully wrapped green and yellow hells. But today there was hope. And hope was like heaven.

When I got home from the cornfields, we were not surprised to see our mother sitting at the table looking flushed by the vapors that rose from the hot tea that she was drinking. We pulled off our coats in the kitchen, pulled our boots off, and limped over to her. Long dreary days were catching up to me.

She looked us over and smiled sadly. The bags underneath her eyes were now permanent markers of her despair. "What's wrong, Brayley?"

Brayley and I exchanged glances.

"Nothing," he answered.

Mother considered his answer and was baffled. Her appetite for her tea suffered. She knew something was wrong and now needed an excuse to talk with him about it. "I need this traded in," Mother said, handing me a pearl necklace. I never asked her any questions when she handed me things that she found at work. I just accepted that her sticky fingers helped put food on our table. "We need food."

I stared at the necklace as I rubbed the tiny beads in my fingers.

"October?"

"Yes. I heard you."

"Okay. Bring back all the food you can get."

Despite the lack of curb appeal, the Plaza was considered an impressive place to us and I loved going there. The Plaza suggested to me that maybe Blue Corn wasn't all that bad. Even before I arrived, I had begun to compose an image in my head. Were it not for the clutter of shops, the flocks of birds scavenging on the ground for leftover crumbs, and the people who came through to trade and buy whatever they could scrape up and sell, it would have been possible not to realize the importance of the Plaza at all. Where I stood I could feel the reach of the fence behind me, and far beyond me on either side, in a silence that seemed to ring my ears. I suddenly became aware of the darkness of the world that I had never known about, too close to me, like a dark figure in the corner of a room.

The sight of the Plaza was then the only comfort there in the world, and there were not many of them in Blue Corn.

I watched as Drew stood near his family's shop throwing breadcrumbs to the flock of birds. The birds were busy shoving their beaks down into the ground romping around digging for a last meal. When I finally stepped onto the Plaza square, I was not surprised to see that the fountain had dried up, the fountain looked just as thirsty as the rest of us. Drew looked up from the birds with his fingers still outstretched.

He smiled at me and looked me over. He watched me intensely to see what I was going to do. My face grew hot, and I hurried into the trade shop to avoid his gaze.

Sister Mary was not alarmed when I walked into her shop. I was no stranger. My family and I were always here to trade in goods. My eyes gazed over the secondhand trinkets and the dusty antiques. Too many to count. They lined the shelves which extended throughout the dimly lit shop. And here I was, cheeks flushed and eyes bright, thinking about Drew. How he had noticed me. Maybe I wasn't invisible to him after all.

Sister Mary considered me. A cloud of remarkable force blew in my face as Sister Mary smoked a long brown pipe and rocked in her chair. She smiled at me revealing yellowy, rotten teeth and her face was filled with crevices and cracks as deep as the bowels of Earth. It was a rumor that she didn't always look like this. That she was a beautiful lady with flowy hair down her back, glowing skin, and beautiful eyes. I wondered what her story was.

"Why hello darling," she purred.

"Hi, Sister Mary."

"What can I do for you today, sweetheart?"

"I just have one thing."

"Well, let me see what you got."

Sister Mary was one of the few people in Blue Corn that dealt with me, so I gladly handed over the pearl necklace and she responded by reaching into her pocket and handing over a crisp twenty dollar bill. "Thank you."

"How are you holding up?" I shrugged. She reached out her wrinkled hand and placed it reassuringly on my arm. "God bless you dear. You'll find your way."

I nodded. She smiled as if she knew a secret that I hadn't been told.

I couldn't help but make my way over to the Keegan's shop. I just wanted to see him, and I was excited when I saw him behind the counter.

"Hi," I said to him. "Can I get some sugar?"

Drew leaned towards me and stared at my mouth with curiosity. The same curiosity that killed so many cats. The temptation for the first bite. He opened his mouth to speak but then hesitated as he set his lips instead for a smile that melted my heart. His sparkly green eyes made my knees weak. "Sugar? Must be a special day?"

"Yes," I couldn't tell him about the pearl necklace.

"Is there anything else I can get you?" he asked.

I stared at him, not wanting to get sidetracked, but getting more distracted every second I stared into his perfect face. "No thank you."

He went off to the back to fill my order and all of Blue Corn was plunged into darkness again. I sighed and leaned against the counter. Beside me pieces of delicious looking sweets were on sale. My father could never afford to buy us sweets. I smelled the air and traces of chocolate kissed my nose. Drew came back carrying a brown paper sack in his arms. The muscles on his arms tensed and bulged underneath the weight. I looked away and was suddenly glad that my dark skin hid the blushing that would've been so obvious on other people.

"Here you go."

I handed him the money.

"Thank you."

"See you later."

"Yeah, okay."

Brayley was sitting at the table waiting for me. He perked up at the sight of me coming inside. I sat the bags on the table just as Mother walked into the kitchen with a quiet that seemed compounded of gentleness and stealth. She smoothed stray blonde hairs back from her face, making herself neat for us. She reminded me of a tragedy. Eve fallen from grace.

"How was Sister Mary honey?"

"Good," I said, handing her the rest of the money. "I think it's about time the Elders gave the place to someone else though."

My mother stared at me. "Do you ever listen to me?"

"I thought it'd be a good idea if we started saving money. You never know what we might have to buy."

My mother sighed. "That's not your decision."

"I'm sorry."

"All the money that we have has to be used for food and for offering," Mother said.

"We have food and you gave the offering for this month, right?"

My mother nodded. "Yes, offering comes every month, if you've forgotten."

"Well, Josef sends you money every week."

"Brother Josef," my mother corrected me.

I started to unload the bags.

"Thank you October for thinking about us, but I got it. I don't want you trying to be an adult right now. You'll have your time. Trust me."

"Mother, pretty soon I'm going to be forced into a marriage and a life that I don't want. It's going to happen and there's nothing you can do to stop it."

"You're not forced."

"Yes we are. I don't want to get married. I don't want to be assigned a job, and I don't even think I want children."

"It's not as bad as you think."

"What if the Elders assign me to someone I don't like?" I asked.

My mother shook her head. "That's how it is. People rarely get married to the person they want. They're blinded by their own lust to see the plan that God has for them," Mother took note of my unconvinced expression. "You'll grow to love them."

"You have no choice but to love them," I muttered.

After a moment, Mother's attention was drawn to the insides of the bag. "This must've cost a fortune. Why would you buy chocolate?"

"I didn't buy chocolate."

My mother corrected me by pulling out a big chocolate chip cookie. "You didn't buy it?" I shook my head and she set the cookie down on the table carefully. "You have to take it back, October. I can't believe you would do this. I thought I taught you better-"

I threw my hands up in defense before she could accuse me of doing such a thing. "I didn't steal it! Drew must've given it to me."

Mother raised an eyebrow at me. "Brother Peter's son?" I nodded. She stared at the cake contemplating. "Well, that was nice of him-"

"October should keep it," Brayley interrupted.

Mother closed her mouth and smiled. "Okay. October, be sure to thank him tonight," She pointed for me to hand her a towel as she began to prepare dinner. "So Drew, huh?"

"Drew, what?"

"October, I was seventeen once," A smile crept on her lips. "When I was in school, I had the biggest crush on his father."

I raised an eyebrow at her.

"Yeah, and on Assignment day I thought Brother Peter was going to be assigned to be my husband, but he wasn't," Mother said.

"Were you upset?"

"Absolutely," she said but then smiled to herself. "Your father was notorious for his curious mind. Cleansing never did keep him long so I knew he was going to be trouble." I didn't know whether I should defend my father or accept that she was right. My mother looked at me with a twinkle in her eyes. It happened every time she talked about him. "But I knew he was the kind of trouble that I needed."

CHAPTER 3

Whereas the cornfields represented the heart and soul of the community, the church was the head. It was grand and the most gorgeous building in the community. While all the other buildings had been built squat and thrown together, the church had been built with a vision and a purpose. A long white steeple extended out to the sky. A mixture of pillars and stained glass was the backbone of the church. Beside the church was the cemetery. It was massive, probably because it was where everyone in Blue Corn was buried. The church's backyard was where we held evening worship.

Tonight was no different. Like a usual night, Genevieve, Cora, and Raven were leading the songs. Genevieve was the front singer while Cora and Raven backed her up. Their voices waded over the crowd like a spell. Everyone danced as if they were enchanted. Zan played the guitar in the back, and Drew played the drums. I watched him as he played. He seemed to be at peace banging against the drum set. Sweat glistened on his forehead, and his jaw clenched as he focused on what he was playing.

Nikki nudged me. "Stop staring."

"I was just watching," I mumbled.

Nikki chuckled. "Sure."

I moved my gaze just as Drew looked out over the crowd. I couldn't tell if he had seen me. I hope he didn't. I caught Genevieve glancing at me. She smirked behind the microphone and belted out more vocals. I rolled my eyes. She knew how to get under my skin.

"Hey, October!" Brayley said, running up to me with Nadia at his side. I looked down at their interlocked hands, and my stomach dropped.

"Brayley, take your hands off of her," I growled at him.

"What's wrong?" he asked.

I stepped towards him and tore his hands away from Nadia.

"Hey!" he shouted.

"You can't do that!" I yelled at him, catching the attention of some of the others. I glanced at Nikki, and her eyes were wide with worry.

"What happened?" my mother asked, running over to us. She placed a hand on Brayley's shoulder in a protective manner.

"He was holding her hand," I said, nodding at Nadia, who had her head hung low.

"I'm sorry," Nadia mumbled.

My mother looked around. She bent down and whispered into Brayley's ear. He nodded. He glared at me and stalked off.

"They don't understand," my mother said, not angrily but firmly

"Well, that's the kind of thing that's going to get them in trouble," I said to her. "Whether they understand or not."

My mother pursed her lips and turned her attention to Nikki. "Good evening, Nikki. Sorry for the misunderstanding."

Nikki nodded. "They're just kids. They'll learn from their mistakes."

My mother nodded in agreement. She gave me one last glare before leaving.

"It wasn't that big of a deal," Nikki said after she left.

"Yes, it was."

As the music died down, Josef finally got on stage. Genevieve and the other singers moved over to the side to allow him to take center. Drew and Zan remained in their places as Josef took to the microphone. The crowd quieted down at his presence on the stage. All eyes were on him.

"Good evening Blue Corn," he said into the microphone.

"Good evening," we repeated back to him.

"Now I can see you all are enjoying yourselves, but our true enjoyment is from Him," Josef preached. The crowd cheered. Every word he said they soaked it up. "We give glory to God. May he continue to bless our covenant community. There is no one else like us."

The crowd cheered again. My mother and Brayley stood in front of me. She grabbed Brayley's hand. He smiled at her touch.

"There is no one like us!" the crowd chanted back. I was silent. I glanced at Nikki who chanted along with the crowd. She looked at me and shook her head. I was silent. I wasn't a part of this, and I didn't believe in any of it.

Josef held his hands out to silence them. The crowd quieted down. "Let's pray."

We all got down on our knees. I bowed my head. I stared down at the grass and listened to Josef as he continued to preach.

"God, continue to bless our people. May they keep your prayers in their heart and serve out of what they know is right…"

I moved my eyes up from the grass to the stage to see that Josef had his eyes closed too. Drew was kneeling beside his drum set. For a second, he moved his head up. His eyes were no longer closed and he was staring straight at me. My breath caught in my chest. We stared at each other completely oblivious to the fact that Josef had stopped praying. He cleared his throat. I looked over at him, and he glared at me. I looked away as the others began to get up from the ground. I looked back at Drew, and he wasn't staring at me anymore.

"Bless us dear lord to keep our eye on you. For all other distractions will only lead to death," Josef said, catching my eye. I looked away.

"Come on October. Dance with us," my father would urge me. He would dance with Mother during the evening worship. This was the only time that I felt like he was a part of Blue Corn. He would spin her around, and she would giggle until she stumbled from being dizzy.

Brayley would urge me too by grabbing for my hand. He loved to dance like our father. I couldn't dance so I didn't like to dance. There was no use in embarrassing myself. I was embarrassed enough.

"Holy be his name!" my father would repeat after everyone.

I would laugh and after, he would be able to convince me. I remembered that the feeling of jubilation didn't come from praising some unknowable God. It came from dancing with my father. A man I loved. Our laughter was spiritual and cleansing to the soul. Not Josef's fake sermons.

"Hi," a voice said beside me.

I was sipping from a cup of water. The other refreshments were cookies baked by the women in the community. I looked to see that it was Drew.

"Hey," I said to him. I watched him as he reached for a cup and poured himself a glass of water.

"You don't want to dance?" he asked, gesturing to the crowd.

"No," I said, watching the others. Flailing arms. Shouts to the sky. It was like something out of a horror show. "I'm not much of a dancer."

"You seem like you could keep a beat. I thought I saw you tapping your foot up there," he said and smiled. I looked away happy that he couldn't see me blush. So he did see me after all.

"Well, you're a pretty good drummer," I said.

"Thanks," he said. "I-"

"October!" a voice interrupted him.

I turned to see that it was Josef.

"Good evening, Brother Josef," I said to him.

"Good evening. How are you?" he asked.

"I'm good," I waited for the next part. The part that always came after.

"How is your mother? Anything I can do to help?"

I feigned a smile. "We're all good."

"Great," he said, placing a hand on my shoulder. I felt myself tense up. I couldn't stand being close to him. He reeked of corn and lies. "May the Lord guide you." I nodded. He turned his attention to Drew. "Drew, you're alright?"

"Yes, Brother Josef," he held up his cup. "Just getting a sip of water."

Josef nodded and glanced at me. "I'll have Sister Celine bring you some next time."

Drew nodded. "Yes sir. Thank you."

Josef looked back and forth between Drew and I. He nodded curtly at me. "I'll be seeing you."

"Yes, Brother Josef," I said. Josef eyed us one more time before leaving. I looked over to see that Drew was watching him. "You should be going back. Wouldn't want you to get in trouble."

Drew placed his cup down. "Yeah. Wouldn't want to miss my solo either."

I chuckled. There would be no solo. The only one who got solos were Genevieve.

"Have a good night," he said walking away.

"I'll try," I called out to him. "Thanks for the chocolate!"

Drew chuckled as he walked back to the stage. I watched as Genevieve walked up to him and started to talk. But he wasn't looking at her. He was looking at me. The butterflies in my stomach grew. I smiled.

If distractions led to death, then I was so dead.

CHAPTER 4

"Maybe we were abandoned for a reason," Brayley whispered to me as he lay down in bed.

That thought crossed my mind before, but I could never tell him that. I had to be strong for him. I would like to think that there had to be a reason that we were left here out of all places. But what was so special about this place?

Brayley watched me tensely and timidly, to see the result of his insinuation. He played with the tangles in my hair twirling them around with his fingers.

I stared back at him. "Maybe Josef doesn't know what he's talking about."

Brayley unwinded the tangle with his finger. He scooted closer to me and kissed me on the nose. "Goodnight, October," he said to me before turning over.

"Goodnight," I said and turned over to face the door. Like a watchdog, I waited for him to fall asleep before I did.

"Keep an eye out for your brother," my father would tell me.

We watched as he played. He was so content in the new life that he had been given. This life fit him. It didn't accept him, but he accepted it.

"I won't let anything happen to him,"

"Good," my father had said. "I wish someone would've told me the same thing."

"You have a brother?" I asked once.

"Yeah," he answered. "But we don't talk anymore. Look out for him. You are all he has here."

"I promise," I remembered telling him.

Later that night, after I found it hard to go to sleep, I ended up watching Brayley as he turned over and moaned. It was as if he was about to wake up, but he didn't. His hands came up and batted the air as if he was fighting something off in a dream. I watched him as he fought for a little while longer, moaning and twisting, and after a final twist, he was still. I figured it was just a bad dream, so I decided not to wake him.

"October?"

I turned to see my mother standing in the doorway. Her hair was wet and so were her eyes. There was a little silence, and then she hesitantly stepped into the room coming to sit on the bed beside me. She put her icy hand on my face. "Did you say your prayers?"

I lied. "Yes."

"Good," she placed a kiss on my forehead. When she pulled back, I could see that sadness was in her eyes. "I miss him."

"What do you think happened to him?"

My mother sighed. "We'll never know."

"Well, I want to find him."

"No," Mother said firmly.

After a moment, I spoke up again.

"Do you think Josef did something to him? What if he escaped?"

"I don't know what to think, but what I do know is that it's too dangerous to go looking for him. If God wanted us to find him, then we would've already."

I looked over at Brayley. He was sleeping on his back, and his chest rose and fell in sync with his breathing. "I think something happened to him at school."

"Yes," Mother sighed. "I'm sorry that you guys are still paying for me and your father's decision. But, when they found you two at the fence, I knew you were mine. You are always going to be part of this community," I looked away from her. That was the part that I feared. "You aren't a mistake. God made you and your brother for me and I loved you from the moment I laid eyes on you," Mother smiled at me. "Your father and I knew Brother Josef and the rest of the Elders wouldn't approve. They didn't even want to keep you two here but when your father and I asked to have you, they didn't say no."

Everyone knew enough about me and Brayley to know that we were outsiders, though we didn't have a choice in whether we wanted to stay. No word had ever indicated who left us at the fence or the whereabouts of our real parents. Our real father and mother chose not to bother with us. Increasingly we saw in our new parents heroes, unlike the others, because they had chosen us. My father and mother made a decision and decided to take us in (for my mother had wanted a child and my father couldn't pass up the opportunity to shake up the community) and their decision had been one of the craziest things to happen in the community. If Josef and the rest of the community had had their way, then they would have left us, six year old me holding a baby outside the fence. *"God made a mistake with you two."* After we heard those words for the first time, we began to put it above the truth, being careful how we approached everything in Blue Corn but not to promise them that we might ever leave to their satisfaction. Once we were brought into the community, we all lived in a state of anticipation. Brayley and I argued about whether our real mother looked like us. Brayley would say, "I know she's like us," and I'd reply, "She isn't. That's why she left."

***

When I woke in the morning, I felt like something in the air had changed. I turned over to find that Brayley's side of the bed was empty. I rubbed my hand over the spot where he laid, and it was cold. I touched my nose to his side of the bed, and I could smell his friction. I was usually up before him. I must have overslept.

I swung my legs off the side of the bed and pulled on my dress. I smoothed my skirt with my hands. The dress was gray, with a dull shine. It had short sleeves and no collar. "What a lovely dress," I wished to hear some day or perhaps a "You look very well." Either would do. Personally, the weather outside was always too cold for dresses, but we had to wear them. Josef didn't allow girls to wear pants. I slipped on my oversized worn boots before leaving the room.

When I walked into the kitchen, I saw that Brayley was buttering a piece of toast. Our mother would usually be sitting at the table with him, but this time she wasn't.

"Goodmorning," Brayley smiled politely.

"Morning. Where's Mother?"

"She's still in her room," he answered.

I turned and walked back out of the kitchen, down the hall, to her room. The door was ajar, so I peeped my head inside. I found her sitting in bed. Her back rested against the headboard. She stared at the wall in front of her.

"Mother?" She didn't answer. She kept staring at the wall. "Are you okay?" Still no answer. I stepped into the room. The curtains were pulled over the windows plunging the room into darkness. Like a tomb. "Mother?" I stood at the side of her bed. She stared at the wall with a blank look.

"I'll be down in a second," she said, never tearing her eyes away from the wall. It reminded me so much of that day.

How I remember the day that my mother realized that my father wasn't coming home. Her hands and feet must have ached. Her heart must have burst. I remember how red and twisted her hands looked, lying in her lap, and how she had pressed her lips together. I remember that, as she sat in the wooden chair that was in the dark living room, staring at the floor, sustaining our stares, her happiness had disappeared.

When she finally looked at me, something wasn't right. There was something wrong with her eyes.

I watched her face, startled by the sudden awareness of me watching her.

"Go talk to him," Nikki whispered to me. She stared at Drew for a second longer, then looked back at me. "He's looking at you."

I made a face at her before getting up from my desk and making my way over to him. The closer I got to him the more nervous I grew. It was like my feet were moving at a faster pace than my mind. In my mind, Drew was so far away, but in reality, I was already standing at his desk. Suddenly, a sharp embarrassment came over me as he laid his gorgeous eyes on me. I forced a smile and slid my hands into my pockets to keep my balance.

"Hey," Drew said.

"Hey," I said. I looked down at the floor as I realized that I was starting to sweat, and my mouth was dry. I looked back up at him, and he was still staring at me. There was astonishment in his face. Neither doubt nor hesitation. There was only astonishment. What did Drew see when he looked at me? A girl with wooly hair, a girl with big lips, who liked to hang around the cornfields, feet on the ground with my eyes towards the sky and my dark skin radiating from me. Did he think I told lies? Did he think I could keep secrets? If someone asked Drew about me, what would he say?

"I baked more cookies," he said.

I smiled. "I'm sure I'll have to buy some this time."

He laughed. "I think I can manage slipping you a few more."

I stared at him. No one here ever tried to be nice to me. I didn't think the others were trying to be rude. It was just difficult to care for something that had no value to them. Drew smiled at me. There were so many things I could have said to him sitting here in this room surrounded by a world that I would never be a part of, but I didn't. I couldn't. "Have a good day, Drew," I said.

"You too, October," he said, smirking.

I walked back to Nikki feeling proud of myself.

"How did it go?" Nikki asked me.

I looked back at Drew who was now busy talking to Zan. "He's nice."

"What are you doing?"

I looked over to see Genevieve watching me from a distance. Usually her stare would make me look away. But today, I didn't. She walked over to me, and the room went quiet.

"I asked you a question. What do you think you're doing?" Genevieve asked.

I scoffed. "None of your business."

Genevieve huffed. She rolled her eyes and flipped her dark hair all at the same time. I scowled at her. She probably practiced how to do things simultaneously. "Who do you think you are? You can't just go up to Drew like that. He's not one of you. Drew is a Saint."

"Wh..Wh..What's your problem?" Nikki stammered. Sometimes when she got nervous, she stuttered. Tiny echoes of words that repeated itself over and over. So much sometimes it was best that Nikki didn't talk when she was angered. I remembered as a kid, it would go on for minutes. I remembered that she wouldn't talk for hours at a time as the echoes irritated her mouth and made her bite her lip shut. One time she bit her lip so hard that her mouth bled.

"Learn how to talk, Ginger!" Raven snapped. I hadn't even noticed her walk up beside Genevieve, but now they were both glaring at me.

"Leave her alone! You came over here for me!" I jumped out of my desk with my fists at my sides. I wasn't usually a violent person, but Genevieve was the only person who took me there. "Why are you so worried anyways?"

"Drew is a Saint," Cora said, appearing beside Raven.

"Yeah, so?"

"So that means he shouldn't be speaking to people like you," Genevieve said. "I will never understand why my uncle let you and your brother stay here."

"Oh yeah?" I stepped closer to Genevieve so that I was inches away from her face. Her eyes bore into my soul, but I wasn't afraid.

"Get out of my face," she snarled.

"Make me."

Suddenly, we were ordered to stop by Sister Jennifer. Her voice cut through the air making both Genevieve and I take a step back from each other without taking our eyes off of each other. Sister Jennifer was so convinced that I was the only guilty one that she beckoned me up to the front of the class and demanded that I account for my actions. I had nothing to account for and so I was forced to remain calm for the sake of my pride. She called my behavior out of place, sinful and tainting the others.

We all knew what was next. I could feel everyone's eyes on me as Sister Jennifer was about to make her point to embarrass me. I focused my eyes on the floor and dared myself not to cry. Not because it wouldn't hurt but because I wouldn't let them see me cry.

This wasn't my first punishment, and it wouldn't be my last At the mere thought of the wooden paddle, I braced myself.

"You better not move," she warned me.

***

During lunch, Nikki didn't bother to engage in any small talk, but a familiar face popped up at our table. My stomach flipped. Nikki and I exchanged glances, eyebrows raised. Drew shifted uncomfortably as he waited for us to say something to him. When we didn't, Drew hesitantly sat down beside Nikki and said, "You have lovely red hair."

"Thanks," Nikki glanced over at me, eyebrows still raised.

"Shouldn't you be sitting with the other Saints?"

"I figured you wouldn't mind."

I didn't, but that didn't matter. I looked back noticing some of the other students, particularly the girls, staring at our table. One group caught my attention fully. That was Genevieve and the others. Raven and Cora were busy flirting with Zan and the other Saint boys while Genevieve scowled at me. I smirked at her and turned back to Drew and Nikki.

"What's up with her?" Drew asked.

I shrugged.

"Genevieve's jealous that you're sitting with us," Nikki answered.

"Really? Why?" asked Drew.

I shrugged.

"Because she likes you," Nikki answered.

Drew's lip curled up in one corner. He made a little gesture with his finger connecting me and him. "They think you and me-"

"That's against the rules," I said quickly, and that's when I saw the flash of light. The two of us posed in an endless succession of temptation-frantic, rapid, images that produced a flickering illusion of movement and fire. The hot and dangerous aromas of our twisted clothes. We flickered while our bodies melted into one. I clenched my jaw to keep my emotions from betraying me. "Girls and boys can't date. We're not allowed to submit ourselves to such temptation."

Drew winked. "I won't tell if you don't."

I blushed.

"Well, that's never stopped some of us," Nikki muttered, hinting to Zan.

"You have a hard time staying out of trouble," Drew said, hinting to earlier. "Although I think it gives them pleasure to see you fail."

I rolled my eyes at the mention of the others. "Yeah, especially Josef. Just more reason for him to want me out of here."

Nikki didn't say anything, but Drew smirked again. "Obviously you're the last thing he cares about. We all can see that. Have you considered standing up against him?"

"Me?" I pointed at myself not that I wanted to or would but because I couldn't believe what Drew was saying.

"Everyone knows what happened to your family, October," Drew said. "We may act like it, but we aren't oblivious. You have more support than you think."

I wiggled my finger at him. "I'm not starting anything I can't finish."

"Who said you wouldn't be able to finish?" Drew asked.

"Are we seriously talking about this here?" Nikki asked, cutting us off. The question was abrupt, and her tone was fearful, because no one dared to talk about rebellion. "If someone hears us, we'll be reported and punished. No worse. You know what happens to heretics."

Death happened to heretics and not the merciful kind.

I remembered the smell of burning embers. Charred pieces of clothing fell to the ground like leaves falling off trees. My father placed his hand around my shoulder, moving me closer to him. I could feel his body shake against mine.

"We are here to carry out the will of God!" Josef's voice roared over us. "Anyone who is not in line with God's word must be taken care of. We must weed out the weak. The heretics. We must confess our sins and pray for God's mercy."

I stared at the burning body. What could they have done to deserve this?

"We must pray. For our God is merciful to the obedient and vengeful to the unjust."

My father spoke of rebellion sometimes, and when he did mention it to us, my mother would wince with irritation. Brayley and I were accustomed to this. I would like to think that my father planned a great escape for us but perhaps it was just for him and then that would explain his disappearance.

Drew and I stopped our conversation immediately because Nikki was right. The Guards, our so called protectors, were always lurking around the corners. They were more like spies. Looking for anyone not following the rules. The word as Josef called it. Josef must have known people would rebel, and I just got a gut feeling that me and my father weren't the only ones who hated Blue Corn.

***

Brayley and I were heading home from the cornfields when in the distance I saw something flickering on the ground. A light or maybe something else. I squinted my eyes for a better look.

"What's that?" I asked, pointing to it. Brayley squinted his eyes as well trying to see what had caught my attention. I sped up.

"Wait!" Brayley called after me trying to keep up.

I ignored his calls and continued towards the mysterious light. It was hope. I could feel it.

"What is it?" asked Brayley, coming up behind me.

I reached out and put my finger on the light. It was tangible. A hope that had just become real. I picked it up and showed it to him. "It's a key."

CHAPTER 5

A week after I discovered the key, Blue Corn had four days of heavy rain. The kind of rain that could wash away sins. Although we all had them, my sins had been weighing heavy on my mind. The constant interruption of how dangerous it was that I was keeping a secret this big. The constant looking over my shoulder. The continual awareness that I now held some sort of power in my hand. I didn't know what to do with it.

"What are you going to do with it?" Brayley asked one day after coming from the cornfields. He had noticed that I had been quiet that week. I was thinking too much.

"I don't know."

The rain had given us four days of rest. Four days to figure out what it was I needed to do with that key.

I decided to see Drew.

"Are you sure about this?" Nikki asked me on our way to the Plaza. I had told her about the key right after I had found it. She didn't know what it was for but warned me that I should be careful with it.

"He's a heretic," I said to her. "I think."

Nikki raised an eyebrow at me and gave me a look. "What makes you think the community's golden boy can be trusted? Because he sat with us?"

She had a point. Drew hadn't given us a reason to trust him besides the fact that he had chosen to sit with a couple of Sinners instead of his fellow Saints. What if him sitting with us meant nothing at all? But what if it meant everything?

"Don't you remember?" I asked her. "Josef killed his mother."

"Of course I remember," Nikki said. "Josef has killed a lot of people."

"I just have a good feeling about him, okay?"

"Just because you like him?" Nikki said. "October, what if you're wrong? You have something that belongs to our leader. Do you know how much trouble we would be in if he knew you had it and I knew and I'm not telling."

"I'm not wrong," I said to her. "Don't you trust me?"

Nikki sighed and rolled her eyes. "Fine."

"Then there's no problem," I said. "If all else fails, I take the blame."

"You know I wouldn't let you do that," Nikki said.

I opened my mouth to object but decided against it. This was always a debate between Nikki and I. With all the wrongdoing I did,

I didn't need anyone to go down with me. But Nikki was dead set on not letting me go down on my own.

When we walked inside of the shop, I saw that Drew was busy dusting off the tables. I began to wave my hand to get his attention, but then I stopped. The muscles in his arms were tense, and his concentration was so focused. Nikki nudged me. Finally, he looked up and laid his eyes on me. The corners of his mouth turned up in an inquisitive smile. His green eyes pierced me. I smiled back. I glanced at Nikki and saw that she was wiggling her eyebrow at me. I looked back at Drew.

Drew stopped dusting and walked over to us. "What's wrong? You guys need something?"

"No. I wanted to show you something," I said, pulling the key out of my pocket and showing it to him. "I found this near the cornfields." He took it and examined its weird shape. "Have any idea what it unlocks?"

Drew shook his head and handed it back. As I grabbed the key, our hands brushed against each other. His hands were warm. I looked up at Drew, and he was watching me to see what I was going to do. I pulled my hand back and acted like nothing had happened, but on the inside, I felt a match light underneath me.

Suddenly, the front door opened, and Drew's quiet giant of a father stepped in. I shoved the key into my pocket just as Brother Peter saw us. I wasn't quite sure if he had seen it, but his eyes glanced at my pocket and then stared up at me.

"Hi, Brother Peter."

"It's nice to see you guys," Brother Peter said to me and Nikki. "How is everything?"

"Fine," Nikki and I said together.

Brother Peter nodded and then placed a hand on Drew's shoulder and squeezed it. He disappeared into the back.

"How would something like this end up near the cornfields?"

Drew shrugged. "I don't know. But I guess that's for you to find out."

Nikki looked uneasy. "I think you should've left it where you found it. You're going to get in trouble."

"I'll only get in trouble if I get caught."

"And we won't let that happen," Drew said.

Our eyes locked with each other. I could imagine that I gasped in shock. In those moments of pure temptation, something passed between us. A warm feeling washed over me, and I knew that he had passed the test. I could trust him. I heaved a sigh of relief. It wasn't easy finding people to be on my side.

***

After dinner, we sat in the living room. Brayley and I played a round of chess. My father had taught me when I was younger, and I had taught Brayley.

"Never let them see you sweat," I remembered my father saying across the chessboard. I would study him as he studied the board.

"I can tell you're sweating," I joked.

"Really?" he would say.

"I can see it too," my mother would joke from the rocking chair. Brayley would be sitting right in front of her feet.

My father would laugh. His laugh filled the room. Back then, he looked so young. He always had that look.

We were only joking. We could never see when he was sweating. We really never knew what he was thinking.

Our mother was in the rocking chair knitting. Today was one of her sad days. She had been quiet the entire night, and she hadn't joined us for dinner.

"I'm beating you," Brayley said.

"Not for long," I said, but I was losing focus on the game as I began to think about the key. I wanted to know where it had come from.

"Mother?" Brayley turned to her.

She smiled at him. "Yes, Brayley?"

"Maybe after me and October finish, we could play a game?" Brayley asked her.

"You know I would love to, baby, but I'm tired tonight. I will play with you tomorrow if the Lord permits," Mother said.

"Yes, Mother," Brayley said and sighed.

Suddenly, the radio clicked on and like always we stopped what we were doing to listen.

"Good evening, Blue Corn," he said. The sound of his voice rolled off the radio and filled our house. Even though he wasn't physically here, I could feel his presence all around us. "I just wanted to remind everyone tomorrow is Cleansing. As you know, it's mandatory for Sinners. Have a good night."

I couldn't help but roll my eyes at the unfairness. "He doesn't have to remind us every time. It's not like we're going to forget."

"Blessed be the meek," Mother said sharply to me.

"Sorry, Mother."

***

Everyone in the house was asleep as I laid in bed staring into the darkness with the sound of Brayley's breath in my ear. I should have been asleep too, but my mind wouldn't shut off. I couldn't stop thinking about my father. I knew I would never be able to accept the fact that he was gone. It all happened too quickly and too suddenly. I needed proof if I was going to believe that he just left without telling anyone. Until I got that proof then the thought of where he could be would never leave my mind. I needed to know for sure if the memories of him were all that I had.

My bedroom door was ajar, and I could see a sliver of light from outside of my door. I got out of bed as softly as I could to not wake Brayley, and I walked over to the door. I opened it and looked down the hall to my mother's room. The light was coming from her room. I tiptoed down the hall to her door. I peered inside to see that she was laying on her side, so she couldn't see me.

"Mother?" I called out to her. She didn't answer. I pushed the door open and walked inside. A candle was lit on the nightstand beside her bed. I walked over to the side that she was facing to find that she was asleep.

The curtains to my mother's room fluttered slightly. I walked over to the window to see that it was partly open. I closed it and turned to leave but stopped when I noticed the light. Our house was the closest to the woods, and I could see a small light emanating from the trees. I squinted to get a better look.

The movement of my mother moved my attention away from the window to see that she had turned over. I looked back at the window, but the light was gone. I blinked as the thought crossed my mind that it could have been a trick of the eye, but I could've sworn I had seen a light. I looked out of the window for a moment longer before turning away.

The candle that was on the nightstand began to flicker. I looked behind me, but I didn't see anyone. I looked back at the flickering candle. I noticed a small bottle on the nightstand. I grabbed it and examined its content. It was filled with small white pills. I wondered where she got them from. I set the bottle down and blew out the candle. Whatever those pills did, I wondered if they helped or hurt. But if I knew anything about the nature of this place, then I knew those pills did nothing good.

CHAPTER 6

The dream always happened the same. I was walking down the aisle of the church. My bare feet were covered with dirt. The lights were dimmed overhead. On the walls, shadows played across the stained glass.

At the end of the aisle, there was Josef standing in the tub. I walked towards him. *Don't. Don't walk towards him. Don't go in there.* The warning came from my conscious mind which knew what would happen once I stepped into the tub with him.

But I couldn't stop moving forward. I let him help me into the tub stepping into the water. I stood in front of him as he smiled at me. I looked down into the tub and saw the water color itself with traces of red ink.

Blood.

Suddenly, I was submerged into the water. The water filled my lungs and I struggled to reach the surface. I blinked until I could see who it was that pushed me down into the water.

My father.

I woke up with a start.

My hands clutched the sheets. My chest heaved up and down. Sweat dripped down my forehead. My stomach was in knots.

I was alone in the room. Brayley must have gotten dressed. I hated Cleansings. With that in mind, I rolled over and got out of bed and pulled on my white robe that was draped at the end of the bed.

Every month, Josef thought it fit that us Sinners be baptized in order to cleanse our souls of impurities. We had no objections, and there was no use in fighting it.

On our walk to the church, my heart filled with anxiety. I hated being in front of the community. They were always watching. We met other people on the road, and my anxiety began to fade as I saw the nervous looks on other people's faces. Today was supposed to represent freedom, but it seemed more like oppression to me.

When we got inside, I spotted Nikki seated with her family towards the back of the church. Her fingers tapped anxiously at her side. She bit her lip and gave me a nervous glance as I passed her.

My mother led us to the front of the church where we took a seat beside her in the front pew on the left side that was designated for Sinners. I looked to the other side and noticed that there weren't many Saints. Just the Elders who were required to come and Genevieve. She had her head bowed, and her fingers clasped in front of her. Her lips moved fast, and I knew that she was praying. I shuddered as I felt like I could hear her whispers in my ear. She was desperate for something.

Suddenly, Josef emerged from the back of the church. He looked at us, acknowledging my mother. She nodded back at him. I looked away so that neither of them saw the look of disgust on my face. Josef went and stood near the tub at the front of the church. He didn't look at us but preferred to adjust his robes while the rest of the Sinners entered the church and sat in the pews.

I looked over at the shadow that stood on the wall of the church. That shadow was Brother Daniel. He was Josef's right hand man. He watched over us and kept us in line as much as Josef did. Whenever he would look at me, I would avoid his stare. He always reminded me of someone. His eyes were so familiar.

When everyone got inside, Josef began the ceremony. "Good morning. It's nice to see everyone on this blessed day. Before we begin, let's pray."

I bowed my head and closed my eyes, mouthing the exact words that Josef said. He said the same thing every month.

"God protect us," he preached. "We pray for our Sinners. For our people are too weak to handle the pressures of your will. Protect them from sin and protect their hearts against all temptations. We are waiting, dear lord, for your wrath to be brought down on mankind. A wrath that has been in the making since the dawn of time. Since the first bite of the delicious apple. Lord, we are your chosen people…"

Someone nudged me on the leg, and I opened one eye to see my mother shaking her head at me.

"Sorry," I mouthed. She pursed her lips.

"…amen," Josef said, finishing up the prayer.

"...amen," we all echoed after him. I glanced at my mother, and she shot me a look.

"Now, let us start with our Saints," Josef turned his attention to the right side of the church. "If anyone would like to receive cleansing, please come now."

I watched Genevieve stand up and walk over to the tub. He looked her over but not with quiet curiosity like the rest of us. Something different. The corners of his eyes softened, and I knew that I had seen that look before. I looked over my shoulder to see if I could see Nikki. I spotted her. Her eyes widened at me as if she had seen it too.

"Pay attention, October," my mother hissed at me.

I turned around quickly.

"Genevieve Walsh," Josef said as he placed his hand on her lower back. "Do you accept God and all his commandments?"

"Yes," she said.

"And do you accept your role as an example for others? To help show them the light and the true path to heaven?"

"Yes."

"Ask God for forgiveness of your sins and prepare to have your mind renewed," Josef ordered.

"God, I have sinned," Genevieve started. "I ask that you forgive me and renew my mind."

Josef lowered Genevieve into the tub. She came back up gasping for air and shivering. "You're forgiven, Genevieve."

Genevieve's devilish smile returned, and she sauntered back over to her seat wiping her face with a towel that an Elder gave her. She glanced at me and sneered. It amazed me at how quickly she turned back into her old self.

When it was my turn, I hesitated at first. My mother nudged me with her feet. I looked up at Josef to see him staring at me. He narrowed his eyes at me, and I moved towards him. I kept thinking about that dream and how I had been submerged in the water. But it hadn't been Josef that had done it so I didn't know why I was so worried.

Josef held out his hand for me to take. I ignored him, grabbing the bottom of my robes as I stepped into the cold water. Josef cleared his throat and placed his hand on my lower back. I shivered and stared at him. He stared down at me, and for a second, I thought I saw his lips curl up in the corner.

"October Harbuck, do you accept God and all his commandments?" Josef asked.

"Yes."

"And do you accept your role to do good here in Blue Corn?"

"Yes."

"Ask God for forgiveness for your sins and prepare to have your mind renewed," Josef recited.

"God, " I started, not wanting to say the words. I had many words to say to Josef's god but not those. "I am a sinner. I ask that you forgive me and renew my mind."

I held my breath as Josef lowered me into the water. The coldness took my breath away, and it felt like my entire body had been woken up. I needed air. I waited another second, but he didn't pull me up. I could feel my lungs starting to burn. I yanked his robe to signal him to pull me back up, but he didn't. I opened my mouth gasping for air but only swallowing water. Finally, he pulled me up out of the water. I came up spitting out water and gulping down air. I drew in a shaky breath. Josef placed his hand on my shoulder. I moved away from his touch. He paused for a second and then smiled. I glared at him.

"You are forgiven, October."

***

"Did you see what he tried to do to me?" I asked my mother once we got back home. My brother glanced at my mother who stiffened.

"October, I don't know what you're talking about," she said.

"He tried to drown me," I said.

"No, October," my mother said, shaking her head. "That's not what happened."

"You're telling me you didn't see anything?" I asked her.

"No."

I looked at Brayley. "You saw it, right?"

Brayley opened his mouth to speak, but then looked at our mother's frustrated expression. He shook his head. "I didn't see anything."

"Liar," I said.

Brayley glared at me before leaving us alone.

"October, just stop," Mother said. "Brother Josef didn't try to drown you. We were all watching. We would have seen that."

"Yeah," I said, rolling my eyes, "because you're so against him, right?"

"October, not right now," my mother said. "Don't try to make something out of nothing."

I didn't respond to her. I watched as she headed into the living room. I followed behind her.

"You know, I didn't feel anything today," I said to her. She sat down in the rocking chair. "The Cleansings. They don't work."

My mother held out her hand to silence me just as the radio clicked on. My mother gave me a look that said we would finish this conversation later, and I looked away.

"Hello, Blue Corn," Josef said over the radio. "Something has happened," his voice reeked of urgency.

"What's wrong?" Brayley asked, appearing in the doorway. He had taken off his robe and was dressed in his buttoned down shirt and pants that were held by his suspenders.

Mother shushed him.

"I have discovered that I am missing a family heirloom," Josef announced. "I'm disappointed that someone from my community would steal from me. I thought I had the trust of everyone here. But I guess I was wrong," Josef paused. "I will search each and every house for what is mine. If you have any heart at all, just bring it back to me. My key is very important to me."

I exchanged glances with Brayley. At the sight of my mother turning to look at us, I held my head down to avoid letting her see my guilt. I started to grow hot. I dug my fingernails into the edge of the couch. Someone placed their hand gently on my shoulder. I looked up to see that it was my mother.

"Are you okay?" she asked.

"I'm fine," I said, releasing my grip on the couch.

"Well, Brayley and I are going to fix dinner," Mother said, going into the kitchen. "It'll be ready in a few." Brayley got up and followed her out of the living room, stopping only to give me a quick glance. I saw him out of the corner of my eye, but I didn't acknowledge him.

His look said it all.

What did I just get myself into?

CHAPTER 7

The panic started after Josef's announcement. The first day Blue Corn was in an uproar. It wasn't a mere accident that Josef's key had been taken. Someone had meant to take the key, and it was a reason it had ended up in my hands. The second day, at school, the news spread rapidly that Josef's search for his key had begun. At the sound of his name my nerves jumped and rattled. The third day everyone's suspicions turned towards me. It was only because they all hoped for someone to blame. It didn't bother me. I would always be their target. In fact, if it weren't for the voice in the back of my head that warned me against making careless mistakes, this incident would have finally come to a close.

"Hands on the desk," Sister Jennifer said all of a sudden, interrupting our lesson. We froze. We all glanced at each other to see which one of us moved first. It was Genevieve. She placed her hands flat on her desk and shrugged at us. She knew she didn't have anything to lose. The others began to follow her lead. I glanced at Nikki who flashed her eyes at me to do the same. I did.

"As you know, Brother Josef's key is missing," Sister Jennifer explained with a watchful eye on us. She began to walk down the aisles looking over each person. "It's a shame that I have to do this, but no one has come forward yet." She stopped at my desk and stared down at me. I didn't have any pockets, but I didn't expect to be treated any better. "Stand up," No one else had to stand up, but instead of making a fuss, I stood up slowly and let her walk around me. She glared at me as she scanned what I was wearing.

"I don't have it," I lied.

"I'll be the judge of that," Sister Jennifer said. I could have easily hidden the key in my boots. I had considered it that morning, but something had told me to leave it at the house. "You can sit," she said when she was done with me. I sat back down and glared at her behind her back.

"What's going to happen if Brother Josef doesn't find his key?" Genevieve asked.

Sister Jennifer considered the question. Her face turned grim, and her mouth tightened. "We're all gonna be punished."

At the end of the three days, the noise had subsided. Josef's search had turned up empty. We had been spared. For now. But I knew it wasn't over.

"Where's Mother?" he asked one day when we had gotten home from the cornfields. Mother hadn't greeted us which meant that she was gone. Brayley walked around the house searching for her. I stood in silence and watched him as a tiny panic started to set in the air.

"She'll be back."

"I hope."

"Just go do your homework. She'll be home soon."

"Okay."

He pulled off his coat and went into the living room. I walked down the hall looking into Mother's empty bedroom. The curtains were pulled apart letting in the light from the day. Her bed was made neatly, and a pair of slippers were placed at the foot of the bed.

I walked inside and sat on her bed noticing how far I sunk into the mattress. I smoothed my palms against her sheets and laid down on my back staring at the ceiling. There was a brown spot right above me. One more rainy day and the ceiling would leak. My foot hit something hard underneath the bed. I sat up and reached under the bed pulling out a small brown chest from underneath it. I got off the bed and knelt down in front of the chest. I opened it.

Inside was a folded blue blanket covered with ducks. I picked it up. It was soft to the touch. I held it against my chest, and for the first time in a long time, I remembered that day like it was yesterday.

A pale hand had held itself out for me to take. I looked up to see them. Their faces at the time had been a mix of lovely sorrow.

Cradled in my arms was a baby. His curly hair peeked out from underneath the blanket, and I could remember wondering what happened to our mother. She had left us to fend for ourselves, and it was now my job to protect him.

I had grabbed the pale hand. Their smile had been so inviting. I don't remember seeing anything else. He held on to my hand tightly because in that moment in reaching for his hand I had reached his heart. His smile had been the chain and the only thing I felt then was gratitude. A strange sense of abandonment, but gratitude all the same.

"You belong to us now," were the first words my father said to me.

I looked back into the chest to see that a small piece of paper had been hiding underneath the blanket. I picked it up and read it.

BLOOMINGTON TIMES

JULY 14, 2005

LOCAL CHILDREN GONE MISSING

The date was what caught my attention. It was from ten years ago which would've been around the time that I had come here.

The sound of the front door shutting startled me, making the newspaper clipping fall out of my hand onto the floor. My mother was home, and I didn't want her to catch me looking through her things, especially things she was purposefully hiding from me. I hurried and grabbed the newspaper clipping and put it back in the chest stopping at the sight of a tiny photo laying at the bottom. I picked it up. It was of me when I was six, a younger Brayley, and a woman. The woman had the same dark skin as me, and her hair was short and curly. I kind of resembled her so did Brayley.

"October?" Mother called from the kitchen.

I shoved the photo in my pocket hurrying to clean up my mess. I pushed the chest back underneath the bed and got up from the floor. I headed out of my mother's room back into the hallway.

"October?" Mother called again. This time she had met me in the hall. "What are you doing?"

"Nothing."

"Were you in my room?" she asked, raising an eyebrow at me.

"I was looking for you. Where were you?"

"I was at the Keegan's shop," she said, walking towards me. I stepped to the side. She eyed me suspiciously. "We have worship in a few."

"I know," I said.

"Go get ready. I'll be out in a few," she said, walking into her room and shutting the door.

I walked into the kitchen to see Brayley with his arms folded against his chest glaring at me.

"What was that all about?" Brayley asked.

I shook my head. "Nothing."

"You were in her room. Did you find something?"

"I said nothing."

"You were snooping."

"Drop it," I said firmly.

Brayley pursed his lips and shook his head.

***

"Look," I said, pulling out the photo from my pocket and showing it to Nikki. She was watching the band on stage, particularly Zan.

She looked over at the photo and studied it. "Where did you get that from?"

"I found it in my mother's room," I said.

"You were snooping?" Nikki asked.

I scoffed. "That's not the point. You think this is my mother?"

"You look like her."

"I know," I said. "Why would my mother have this photo of us? Do you think she got it from the outside?"

"I don't know."

"It's not just that," I said, putting the photo back into my pocket. "I found something else. Something about local children missing ten years ago."

Nikki furrowed her eyebrows in confusion. "What are you saying?"

"What I'm saying is that my parents lied. They told us that we were abandoned at the fence. Nikki, I don't think that's true."

Nikki glanced around nervously. "Then what do you think happened?"

"I think we were taken," I said. "I think Brayley and I were brought here for a reason. I just need to find out why."

CHAPTER 8

In the weeks that followed, Josef came to our house almost every evening. He would eat dinner with us and escort us to worship. He would invite us over to his house, but my mother would always decline. I think she did it for me because when he would come over, she would smile. On occasion, she would slip her hand into Josef's, and they would talk. Everything in her manner suggested that she wanted him. He would smile back, and his face would blush in shyness. Even at church, Josef would ask us to sit in the front. I knew that his actions were leading to something more. The community of Blue Corn was pleased by it. And it seemed like the more time they spent together, the more satisfied everyone else was.

"Are you really going to marry him?" I asked her one night after he had left. I had noticed after dinner they had disappeared into my mother's bedroom. It was so obvious even Brayley could see it.

"Do you have that key?" my mother asked me, avoiding the question. But her avoidance only gave me the answer that I needed.

I shrugged. "I'm pretty sure that key is right under his nose."

"That key is important, October," my mother said. "Whoever has it should just turn it in and spare us all."

"Maybe whoever has it just wants to keep him on his toes. Like he does us."

My mother raised an eyebrow at me. "I think it's dumb. That person is going to be responsible for a lot of bad things happening to innocent people."

"Innocent? I think you're misjudging these people."

My mother shook her head. "And I think you're misjudging Josef. He's not going to let it go."

I smirked. "Well, that makes two of us."

***

Service Day came in late autumn. Every year for a day we were assigned to one of the adults in the community to work for.

"Ready for today?" Drew's voice startled me from my daze.

I peeled my eyes away from the window and looked over to see him standing in front of my desk. His green eyes scanned over my face, and for a second, my soul fluttered.

"I guess. Are you?"

Drew shrugged. He stared down at me. I suddenly became aware that the top button on my blouse had come undone. A peek of skin stuck out and exposed itself. Drew tore his eyes away from my flesh and blushed.

"Who are you hoping to get?" I asked, reaching to button my shirt. Drew's eyes followed my fingers.

"Umm..." he stammered as he lost his train of thought.

"I'm hoping for Brother Corbin," Nikki said, appearing beside Drew. She sat down in her desk. "But they'll never let me be a doctor."

Drew cleared his throat and ran his fingers through his hair in adorable embarrassment. I glanced at Nikki, and she squinted her eyes at me. I bit my lip to hide my smile.

The door opened, and we all looked to see Sister Jennifer walk inside.

"Good luck," Drew said to us before going away quickly to his seat.

"As you know tomorrow is Service Day," Sister Jennifer said walking over to her desk. "The Elders and I have assigned you someone in the community that you will be working for," Sister Jennifer folded her arms across her chest and looked us over. "The Lord blesses those who work. Through work will you find His favor." Sister Jennifer reached behind her and grabbed her clipboard. She started to call the names off the list in alphabetical order.

I didn't have an interest in Service Day. For some reason, it never occurred to me that I would be making a life here. Working. Raising a family. It all seemed unreal to me, but it would be my reality soon. Nonetheless, I was anxious to know who I would be paired with.

"Nikki Duhamel," Sister Jennifer said, reading off of the clipboard. "Sister Lauren."

Nikki glanced at me and gave me a small smile. I knew she wanted to be with Brother Corbin, our community's doctor, but we all knew the Elders wouldn't allow that kind of thing. But at least she got the next best thing. The nurses did about as much as the doctor did. And my mother did like being a nurse.

"October Harbuck," At the sound of my name, I perked up. "Brother Ward."

I gawked at Sister Jennifer. It was like a slap to the face. Brother Ward was the groundskeeper.

"You're kidding me?" I interrupted her at the sound of another name being announced. Sister Jennifer paused and looked up at me.

"No, I'm not," Sister Jennifer said and looked back down at her clipboard. "All decisions are final."

I sat back in my seat, silently fuming to myself.

***

"Maybe it won't be that bad," Nikki said to me.

It was lunch, and I looked around the yard as everyone speculated about what tomorrow would bring for them. I looked over at Genevieve and the other girls. I wasn't surprised when Genevieve was paired with her mother. I cringed at the idea of Genevieve teaching a class. She caught me staring at her, and she laughed. I knew she was mocking me. I looked away from her.

"He's a groundskeeper for God's sake, Nikki," I said to her. "They really think that low of me, huh?"

"Maybe it's not that," Nikki tried to counter it. "I mean, we're paired with people who we're supposed to learn from. Maybe there's something to learn from Brother Ward."

"Like what? How to rake leaves?" I snapped.

Nikki pursed her lips and said nothing.

I didn't mean to snap at her so quickly. I had expected more, but maybe it was my fault for thinking that the Elders even cared enough about me to consider what I wanted. Brother Ward was like part of the shadows. He moved about us being everywhere but nowhere at the same time. We saw him in passing sometimes, cleaning yards, tending to the graves. He always kept his head low. Ears to the ground. He lived in a rundown shack in the woods.

I could remember watching Brother Ward as he painted one of the shops. He hadn't been that much older than me.

"Well, aren't you going to speak?" my father had asked me. "He's not going to bite."

I looked over my shoulder to see him coming out of the Keegan's shop holding a brown paper sack. He nodded to Brother Ward.

"Good afternoon, Ward," my father had said to him.

Ward glanced at my father. "Hey," he muttered underneath his breath. His voice had been deep and rough like it was cut from gravel. I had kept staring at him because for some reason I was fascinated by him.

My father put a hand on my shoulder and guided me away from the shop. I took one more look back at Ward. I had wanted to know more about him.

"There he is," Nikki said, nodding over to the road.

I turned to see Ward walking beside a horse he was leading in one hand and carrying an apple in the other.

"Should I say something?" I asked.

Nikki shrugged. "I guess."

I got up from the table and headed towards him. He didn't notice me until I was a few feet away from him. He stopped the horse and stared at me.

"Hey," I said.

"Hey," he raised an eyebrow at me questioningly.

"I don't know if you remember, but-"

"I know who you are," Ward said. "What do you want?"

"I, umm," I paused for a second because the way that he looked at me made me want to turn back. His stare was intense. I looked down at the ground so that he couldn't see how much I was panicking. "I just wanted to say that tomorrow is Service Day."

"Yeah, so?" Ward asked.

I looked back up into his stare. "The Elders put me with you."

"Are you sure?"

"Yeah," I said.

Ward considered this. He nodded once. "Okay. Well, I'll see you tomorrow."

"Yeah, tomorrow."

The horse neighed and nuzzled his nose against Ward's arm. "Sorry buddy," Ward held the apple up to the horse's lips, and it took the apple whole. Ward looked back at me. "Anything else?"

"Oh. No," I forgot that I was staring at him. "See ya." I turned and headed back to the schoolyard where the others were watching me. Genevieve and the others gawked at me. No one ever spoke to Ward. Their stares didn't bother me. The only person who I wondered enough about to glance over at them was Drew. He was sitting with Zan who hadn't registered that Drew's focus wasn't in the conversation. I could see him staring, but I didn't acknowledge him.

I sat back down in my seat.

"Well, what did he say?"

"There has to be a reason the Elders put me with him," I said.

"Um, yeah," Nikki said as a matter of fact. "He does a lot."

"No," I said. "It's more than just about the job. He's different."

"Different, how?" Nikki raised her eyebrow. "October, he's just a groundskeeper."

"No, I think he's more," I said, glancing back at the road. He and the horse were almost out of focus. "Maybe there is something I can learn from him."

CHAPTER 9

At last came Service Day. My mother knew that I was paired with Ward, and when I had asked her what she thought about him, she simply replied that it would be interesting. I didn't ask any further questions and figured she was just as puzzled about the Elder's choice as I was.

"Be good," my mother said on my way out of the door.

"Always," I said.

The walk to Ward's cabin wasn't more than ten minutes, but I walked slowly. I could hear kids in the distance and thought about how they would have a much better time than I would.

The trail to Ward's cabin winded, and I started along the wood's path. The morning light was bright, and birds jumped out of trees overhead and flew into the sky. Somewhere in the woods the trees began to grow fuller. The canopy overheard was thicker, and the light wasn't as bright. Lush greens were plentiful, and I tried my best to avoid the stumps and fallen branches on the ground. Finally, I came to a tiny space in the woods where the cabin sat. It was buried alongside the trees and bushes as if it had grown along with them. Vines covered the walls, and an eerie feeling suddenly came over me. I stopped at the cabin's front porch. I wanted to turn around, but I knew I couldn't.

At the moment my foot hit the wooden step, a dog began to bark from the inside of the cabin. I paused looking over at the small wind chime that swung slightly. I didn't feel any wind, but I figured a breeze must've blown by and I was too nervous to feel it.

The barking continued as I made my way up the steps to the front door. I knocked on the door.

"Hello?" I called out. There was silence except for the sound of the dog barking. The woods were quiet. I knocked again.

This time I didn't call out. I moved to the front window to see if I could see inside, but the window was covered by half drawn curtains. I could see a couch and a fireplace inside. I squinted my eyes to get a better look, and that's when the door opened. A small brown dog bolted out of the door and up to me as it sniffed at my feet. Ward stepped out and looked back and forth between me and his window.

"Get a good look?" he asked.

"Sorry," I said, moving away from the window. I could feel the dog at my feet pawing at my legs.

"Cassie, get inside!" Ward commanded the dog.

The dog moved away from my feet and scurried back into the house.

"Sorry, she's not used to company," Ward said, walking to the door and pulling it close. He pulled a key out of his pocket and locked it. We never locked our door in the community. We all knew each other, and we doubted anyone would steal from us. I wonder what it was that Ward didn't want people snooping around.

"We're not going inside?"

"No. It's time for work."

"Oh," I said, finally noticing the dirt on Ward's shirt and the mud covering his boots. He had a black streak of dirt on his cheek. He caught me staring and suddenly became aware of the dirt on his face. He wiped at it. "You're usually working this early in the morning?"

"Yes. Sunup to sun down."

"Doing what?"

"Things that groundskeepers do."

"Well, I'm here to help," I said.

Ward nodded. "Follow me."

I followed him around the corner of the cabin to a tiny shed. He opened the door, and he wedged himself where I could see tools were jammed inside. He pulled out an ax, a rake, and a pair of clippers. He handed me the rake.

"So what are we doing today?"

"It's your lucky day," Ward said. "We're cleaning the cemetery."

We walked to the cemetery in silence. The only sound we could hear was the crunching of the leaves underneath our feet. Ward wasn't a talker, and I didn't have much to say or ask him. There was a strange sense of comfort with him.

"It's not that bad," Ward said, finally ending the silence. "The cemetery. It's a good place to think."

He looked back at me as I struggled to keep up with him. I pushed past bushes and ducked underneath low hanging branches. He turned back around, but I could hear him chuckling to himself.

Blue Corn's cemetery was massive. Many of the people buried here had been at the mercy of the Annual Harvest. The names that were carved into the headstones were familiar. All of the previous leaders had received large memorials carved out of white granite. The founding prophet's memorial was the largest. I scanned the rows of headstones for any connection to the names. I saw Drew's mother's name. Alice Keegan.

So this is what death was, I thought. The chilly air and the twisted trees that hung over the graves reached out as if they were guarding the dead.

For a chilling second, I thought about my father being in one of those graves. I wondered if it would have felt different. Maybe it would have felt better if I had gotten to say goodbye.

"When is he coming home?" *I would ask day after day. Night after night we would wait for him. None of us could sleep.*

"I don't know," my mother would say. "He'll be home soon. I just know it." But even back then I could see that she wasn't certain, and from then on, we hadn't been certain about anything else. The only certainty was that he wasn't coming back to us.

"Do you think he's dead?" Brayley had asked.

I had no answer. I remembered my mother crying into the palms of her hands.

"You hold it like this," Ward said. He stood behind me and grabbed my wrist positioning my hand where it should be. I froze. I looked back at him. He smelled like the woods. A mixture of earth and grass.

"Thanks," I said. His eyes moved to my face and stared down at my hands. His hand stayed on my wrist a second longer. My thoughts went to Drew. His golden hair and light eyes. Ward had dark hair and dark eyes. I stiffened and looked away. Ward stepped back. He cleared his throat and went back to pulling weeds that had overgrown around some of the headstones.

"You know they never found my father's body," I said.

Ward didn't look up. "Yeah, I know."

"He didn't leave us," I said. "They're trying to make me feel like I'm crazy."

"You're not crazy."

"Oh yeah?" I said, "Then why doesn't anyone talk about him? About what happened?"

Ward paused. "I don't know. Maybe it's something about what happened you don't want to hear about."

"I think Brother Josef knows what happened."

Ward didn't answer at first instead he went back to pulling weeds. I thought maybe it had been a mistake. Me telling him my suspicions, but being out here in this cemetery, something felt right. Secrets were always better told around the dead. The dead couldn't tell. "I think so too." Ward finally mumbled.

I stopped raking. Ward looked up at me. I smiled. "Maybe they were right with putting me with you."

"Oh yeah, why's that?"

"You know I used to think that this was all my fault. That maybe God was punishing me. Because of who I am. I don't know anymore."

"God isn't punishing you, October. It doesn't work that way," Ward said. "And stop thinking like that. Nothing is wrong with you. You know it's total bullshit what he says, right?"

"Is it?" I asked. "Because being here makes me feel so-"

"Alone," Ward finished for me.

I stared at him. "Where's your wife?"

There was a silence then Ward shook his head. "I don't have one."

"Why not?"

Ward shrugged. "I guess they didn't want to waste a marriage. Besides, no one wants to be with someone like me. Cleaning cemeteries for a living isn't very attractive."

I laughed. "Well at least you're doing something. My mother always said cleanliness is next to godliness."

Ward smiled slightly, and all of a second he was handsome. "It's okay. I don't mind being alone. I have Cassie. She keeps me on my toes," Ward nodded to the small pile beside me. "Keep raking."

"Sorry."

I went back to raking the leaves, stealing chances to glance at Ward. I was struck by Ward's ability to look like this was where he was supposed to be all along. That there was nothing else in the world he craved. He was strong, I could tell. The way his muscles moved underneath his shirt. The way the ripples in his skin snaked and squirmed as he scooped the weeds in a large bag. His strength was palpable like the tension I was starting to feel between us. Perhaps, I had been wrong about him. The thought excited me.

"It gets better," Ward said suddenly.

I looked up from raking the leaves to see that he was staring at me.

"You'll find out what happened to him. I promise. Everything isn't what you think anyways."

"What do you mean?"

"I mean that I knew your father and if you think he would have abandoned you and your family, then you're wrong. That isn't what happened," Ward said.

"Yeah, how do you know?"

"Your father was a heretic. That's true, but he would never leave you here."

"What makes you think that?"

"He told me once," Ward said. "'Nothing mattered more to him than you, October. He would've burned this whole place down for you."

CHAPTER 10

"How well did you know him?" I asked Ward as he walked me home. Service Day was over, and after cleaning the cemetery, we spent the rest of the afternoon cleaning the stables.

"He was around. Him and my mother were friends, so I would see him sometimes at the house. He was different," Ward said. Ward's mother was Sister Mary. I found it odd that I've talked to her many times and she had never mentioned that her and my father had known each other outside of the occasional trading.

"What do you mean?"

"Not crazy different, just different. Like wanting to change this whole place," Ward said. "You seem to be like that."

I looked at him. A small smile played on his lips. "I'm glad they assigned me to you."

"Me too," Ward said.

Finally, we made it to the clearing where I could see my cottage a few yards away. I could see my mother hanging clothes on the line.

"Take care, October," Ward said, turning to leave.

"Wait," I said, reaching out to him. I grabbed his wrist making him stop. He turned to look at me. His dark eyes made me imagine things. I let go of his wrist feeling guilty about thinking of him in that way. "I want to find the truth. About my father. About what happened. Help me."

Ward considered this. He nodded.

"Bye," I said to him.

"See ya, October," he said.

I turned to leave. I could feel him watching me even as I walked up to my mother. She looked at me and smiled.

"You look like you had a nice time," she said, pinning a linen to the line.

I nodded. "I did. It wasn't that bad. He's not what everyone thinks, you know."

"Neither are you," she said smiling. She handed me a basket full of clothes. "Help me with these, would you?"

I took the basket and glanced back in the direction of the woods to see Ward still standing there. He threw up his hand in a wave. I smiled at him.

***

"Is there something you want to tell me?" Nikki asked.

We were standing near the back of the crowd during the evening worship. "About what?"

"About Brother Ward," Nikki said, studying me in a way that told me she was looking for the truth.

"No," I said, trying to hide my smile. "He's nice."

"You liked him, didn't you?"

I snorted. She knew me too well. "I didn't say that."

"You didn't have to," Nikki said.

"There's nothing to say."

"Mhmm," she said. "What are you going to tell Drew?"

"I'm not telling Drew anything," I said. "Nikki, please. Let it go."

Nikki laughed. "Alright!"

"October, I can't find him!" a girl's voice shouted to us. It was Nadia. She raced up to us in a fit of panic.

"Nadia, what's wrong?" Nikki asked.

"It's Brayley!" she cried. "I can't find him! I saw him go with Garrett behind the stage, and when I went to look for him, I couldn't find him!"

Nikki and I exchanged glances.

"Come on! I'll show you!" Nadia said.

I followed Nadia with Nikki close behind me. We followed her behind the stage where it was empty.

"They were here," Nadia said, pointing to a spot on the ground. "And now he's gone."

I knelt down where she pointed, noticing a red mark on a blade of grass. I touched it, smearing it on my fingers. It was blood.

"Is that blood?" Nikki asked.

I blinked as a feeling of sickness came over me. What if he was hurt? Someone placed their hand on my shoulder, and I realized my breath had quickened.

"Come on. We'll find him," Nikki said. "This is a small place, He couldn't have gotten far."

"Look!" Nadia said, pointing in the direction of the church.

My eyes darted over to where she was pointing. It was Garrett. He was walking briskly away from the church. He was tall for his age and twice the size of Brayley.

I hopped up and started running towards him. I had gotten the attention of the crowd as I pushed past some of them, but I didn't care.

"Hey!" I called out to him.

Garrett looked up and backed away but not in enough time to get away from my grasp. I caught the edge of his collar and pulled him close to me.

"Get off!" Garrett yelled, pushing me off of him.

I was about to reach for him again, but Nikki grabbed my arm and held me back. I could feel the heat rising in my chest. "I know you did something to him! Where is he?"

Garrett smirked. "How am I supposed to know where the little darkie is?"

I scoffed in disgust.

"Garrett, you're a monster," Nadia spat at him.

His eyes moved over to Nadia in an intense glare that made her avert her gaze.

"Where is he?"

There was silence as Garrett stared at me. Finally, his lips curled up in the corners. "He's in there," Garrett said, nodding to the church.

Nikki let me go, and I moved past him hurrying up the stone steps. I pulled the doors open. The church was empty except for a single figure sitting near the front of the church. It was Brayley. He held his head down.

"Brayley?" I asked walking up to the pew that he was sitting in. I sat down beside him. He didn't look up. I could hear the tiny gasps as he sobbed silently to himself. I placed my hand on his back. "Brayley, what's wrong?" He didn't answer. I leaned closer, and Brayley scooted away from me slightly. "What did he do to you?" I reached down and placed a finger under his chin pulling his face up so that I could see him.

I gasped.

It was the first time something like that had happened. Brayley had been seven. We had been playing in the cornfields, and I had lost him. As I searched for him in the tall rows of corn, I could hear the sobs. I followed them until I found him on the ground with his hands covering his eyes.

"Brayley, what's wrong?"

"I can't see!" he screamed.

"What?" I said, kneeling beside him. "Let me see."

He let me move his hands away from his eyes. The whites of his eyes were covered with dark specks of dirt. I shuddered and moved away a little.

"October?" Brayley called out to me.

"It's okay," I told him, taking him into my arms. I wanted to cry too. "It's okay."

"They hate us," I remembered him whispering.

"He said he was doing God's work."

I caught my breath at the sound of Brayley's whisper. "Oh God." Brayley's nose dripped blood, and one of his eyes was swollen shut. A cut ran along the side of his forehead and across the bottom of his chin. "He did this to you?"

Brayley nodded. "He said God didn't create people like us."

"You don't believe that, do you?"

"No."

"Good because Garrett can go to hell," I said. "I'm sorry I wasn't there to protect you."

"It's not your fault."

There was silence as Brayley wiped the tears on the back of his hand.

"Come on," I said, standing up. "Let's get you cleaned up."

"Okay."

We walked out of the church to find Nikki and Nadia standing at the bottom of the steps.

"October, something's happening," Nikki said, glancing at Brayley. Her eyes widened.

"What are you talking about?" I asked.

"He's making an announcement," Nikki said.

"About what?"

"I don't know."

I looked at Brayley. "Stay here."

"What's going on?" Brayley asked.

"I don't know," I said. "I'll be back."

Nadia placed a hand on Brayley's arm and nodded. "We'll be here."

Nikki and I made our way back to the crowd. The band had stopped playing. The crowd was watching the stage in awe and fascination. Some people took notice of me and smiled.

"She's here," I could hear some of them say.

I walked to the front of the crowd to see that my mother and Josef were on the stage. "What's going on?" My mother gave me a small smile.

"You're just in time, October," Josef said.

"For what?" I asked, but Josef ignored me.

"I need everyone's attention!" Josef called out to the crowd. The crowd quieted down as Josef dug into his pocket pulling out a tiny box. Josef cleared his throat and knelt down on the ground. He opened the box revealing a shiny ring. My mother gasped along with the crowd. I was speechless. "Sister Lauren, I have admired you from afar. You and I have something special and I don't want to live another day without you by my side."

There was silence as we all waited. My mother glanced at me quickly before turning her attention back to Josef.

"Sister Lauren, will you marry me?"

CHAPTER 11

It turned into a nightmare as the proposal played over and over in my head. My mother's wide smile. Her embrace with Josef. I shut my eyes. I waited for the ground to split. For the sky to open. The prophecy had been fulfilled. The image of a pale virgin engulfed by a charming devil. All around me the crowd praised them in glory.

"This is wonderful!"

"A wedding! Oh my!"

"What a wonderful choice!"

I opened my eyes and watched as Josef paraded my mother in front of the crowd who was still applauding. It was deafening.

Nikki nudged me. "Clap," she ordered. "He's watching you."

"I can't do this," I said, turning to leave.

Nikki grabbed my arm. "He'll see you."

"Nikki, I can't," I said. I could feel the tears coming, and I needed to get away. This was so wrong, and I wanted no parts of it.

I moved through the crowd as they all congratulated me. They were too busy in their blissful ignorance to see the pained expression on my face. I walked over to the church where Brayley and Nadia were sitting on the steps. They were holding hands, but I didn't bother to chastise them this time.

"We have to go," I said to Brayley.

"What was all that about?" The blood had dried around Brayley's mouth.

"Josef proposed to Mother," I said.

"What?" Brayley asked, standing up.

"I need to clean you up," I said, changing subjects. "Let's go."

"But-"

"Brayley, let's go!"

He was taken aback. Nadia's eyes widened. I didn't mean to yell. I wasn't angry. I just didn't know what else to do. Brayley nodded and got off of the steps. He followed me silently. He didn't ask questions as the sobs broke through my parted lips. He walked beside me, and it was the only comfort that I needed.

Once we got inside the house, Brayley sat down at the kitchen table as I gathered up the tools to clean him up: a fresh towel, water, and some alcohol. I sat down in front of him and started to clean his face.

"Did she say yes?"

"Yes."

"You think she loves him?"

"I don't know."

I cleaned the rest of his wounds in silence. Finally, the door opened and my mother stepped in. Her face was flushed.

"Congratulations," I said without looking at her.

"Brayley, what happened to you?" my mother asked, ignoring me. She walked up to him putting her fingers under his chin moving his face up to her so she could get a better look.

"It was Garrett," I said.

"Are you going to marry him, Mother?" Brayley asked.

My mother nodded. She bent down to kiss Brayley on the forehead. "I need to talk to your sister alone."

Brayley nodded. He got up and left us alone. My mother sighed and took the chair that Brayley was sitting in. I watched as she took the ring off of her finger and placed it on the table. She took a deep breath.

"We're moving tomorrow," she said.

"Moving?" I asked. "Where?"

"To Josef's house," she said. "The Guards will be here in the morning."

I gawked at her. She held her head down and closed her eyes. "Is this what you want?" A tear fell from her closed eye down to the floor. "Mother?"

She looked up at me with a tear stricken face. I could see the fear and sadness written all over her face. She grabbed my hand, and we cried together before packing up our things.

***

The Guards arrived at sunrise. Brother Daniel was among them. He stood by the door and waited on us as we scrambled to pack our last few things. With sleep in our eyes, we said our last goodbyes to our home.

Our walk to Josef's house was quiet. The sun hadn't quite climbed its way to the sky's top. No one was on the road. Our footsteps were the loudest sound against the gravel. Brayley slipped his hand into mine. Last night I heard him cry himself to sleep. I wanted to comfort him, but I didn't have the strength to. I was still fuming over what Josef had done. If my father were here, none of this would be happening. Josef would have stayed away from my family, but then again, in the end, Josef always got what he wanted.

I looked over at his face to see that his eye was still noticeably swollen, but it wasn't as puffy as it was before. I squeezed his hand in silent reassurance, and he feigned a smile. As long as we were together, everything would be okay.

Josef's house was impressive. It was surrounded by a wire fence and tall trees. The house was taller than it was wide. It was extravagant. Everything was too big. There was a long porch that wrapped around the house, and the windows were too tall. The landscape surrounding the house was too green. The fountain that was in the middle of the lawn spewed water that was too clear. Everything was too perfect. There wasn't an imperfection in sight.

A hand squeezed my shoulder. I looked back to see my mother standing behind me.

"It's beautiful, isn't it?"

I gave her a small smile in return and placed my hand on top of hers.

We walked up the porch steps which moaned under our weight. The front door opened for us. It was Sister Celine. She nodded at us.

"Welcome," she said. The permanent bags underneath her eyes told me that Josef was overworking her like he did the rest of us, maybe even more.

We stepped into the house to find that it was just as perfect on the inside as it was on the outside. The dark hardwood floor was polished, and the high ceiling was adorned with a bright chandelier. The front part of the house was wide with each end opening up into a different area of the house. A wide staircase took up most of the front of the house which ran up to a second floor.

"You made it!" Josef said, coming out of what appeared to be the living area to the right. He walked over to us and grabbed my mother's hand. He kissed it and smiled at us. "Welcome to my home!"

"We're glad to be here," my mother said.

"Come," Josef said, moving towards the living area. "Let me show you around. Brother Daniel, would you take their things upstairs, please?"

Brother Daniel, who was standing beside Sister Celine, nodded.

Josef led us to the right where we walked inside the spacious living area. A large window made the room lighter. The fireplace and the antique furniture made the room comforting. The carpet was a rich dark green color, and there was a tall grandfather clock in the corner of the room.

"That clock was built by my great-great grandfather," Josef said. "It still works and it's the oldest thing in the house."

We left the living area and moved to the left area of the house that led into the kitchen. The walls were lined with a stove, a sink, and cabinets filled with porcelain plates and glasses. Near the back of the kitchen was a door that led to the outside and a pantry door was in the corner of the room to the right of the refrigerator. We moved deeper into the kitchen, and it led into a back room where a large dining table was placed in the center of the room. The dining table was decorated with tall candles and more porcelain plates and cups.

"Dinner is usually at six," Josef said. "Sister Celine cooks the best meals."

We returned to the front part of the house and were led to a door that was to the left of the staircase.

The door opened into a study. I could tell this room was used. The coffee table in the middle of the room had papers strewn over it, and the chair and couch cushions had indents on them. A bookcase ran up to the top of the ceiling to the left of a desk.

"I spend most of my time here," Josef said.

"Josef, you have a beautiful home," Mother said.

Josef walked up to her, putting his hand in hers. I had a sudden urge to gag. "We have a beautiful home."

We left the study and went back to the front of the house where we followed Josef up the stairs. Once we got up the stairs, I froze at the sight of the paintings that were placed on the walls. Beside every room was a portrait of who I assumed were the Walsh family.

Josef walked up to the door beside the portrait of a man with a thick brown mustache and stern eyes. The portrait was labeled as William Walsh.

"October, this is your room," he said, placing his hand on the doorknob. He opened the door to reveal a clean and spacious bedroom. The walls had floral wallpaper. A single bed with a green bedspread sat against the wall underneath a painting of a woodsy landscape.

"Wow," I said, stepping further into the room. A door to the bathroom was in the corner of the room opposite to the bed. Next to it was a tall wooden wardrobe and a dresser with a mirror. I walked over to the window that was on the wall near the side of the bed. I looked out to see Josef's backyard which had a patio with tables and chairs.

"How do you like it?" Josef asked.

I looked at him and nodded. "Thank you," I said.

"It's the least I can do. We're going to be family after all," he said smiling.

Brother Daniel appeared in the doorway carrying my bags. He walked in, placing them at the foot of my bed.

"Brother Daniel will be here most of the time except nights. Anything you need you can ask him as well. He knows as much about this place as I do," Josef said.

I glanced at Brother Daniel. He caught my eye and gave me a curt nod.

"Brayley, I think it's your turn," Josef said. "Ready?"

Brayley smiled and nodded. "Ready."

Josef left the room, and my mother and Brayley followed, leaving me with Brother Daniel. I stared at him because there was something familiar about him. I just couldn't figure out what it was.

I found my father one day sitting on his bed staring down into the palms of his hands. Only when I had walked into their room did I realize that it was a photo that he was looking at.

"You okay?" I had asked him.

"Yeah," he said quickly. He looked up at me and sniffed, drawing back the tears that had gathered in his eyes. "Everything's fine."

"Something's wrong," I said, sitting beside him. I looked down at his hands. "What's that?"

I remembered he had shown me the photo. It was of two young boys. They had the same blue eyes. The same boyish smile.

"It's someone's birthday today," he said. "Someone special to me."

"Do I know them?" I asked.

"No," he said and planted a kiss on the top of my head. "But you will one day."

"Well, if you need anything let me know," he said. "I'm around."

"Thank you," I said as I watched him leave. He walked out of the room. I walked over to the wardrobe and opened it. It was already filled with clothes and new shoes. I pulled out a dress and held it against my body. The inside of the wardrobe had a mirror hung on the door, and I looked to see that the dress was a perfect fit.

For a second, I imagined myself wearing the pretty dress. My hair was done in a way that allowed it to flow in the wind. The air gliding over my skin and making me feel as light as a feather. The image faded, and I felt like I had been floating.

I hung the dress back into the wardrobe and closed it, noticing a white square laid on the dresser. I picked it up to find that it was a piece of paper that had been scribbled on with an elegant handwriting.

October,
I hope you like it here. This is a new beginning.
-Brother Josef

"I had a note too," a voice said from the doorway. "And new clothes."

His voice startled me. I looked up to see Brayley standing in the doorway. He was looking down at his feet, and I noticed he had on a different pair of shoes. "Why do you have those on?"

"The clothes are for us," Brayley said.

"And how do you know that?" I asked, putting the note back on the dresser.

"Everything fits perfectly," he said. "It's like he knew we were coming."

"I still don't like it."

Brayley shrugged. "Well, we're here. Brother Daniel says it's nice to see the house full again."

"Don't talk to him."

"Why not?"

"Because we don't know him," I had no real reason not to talk to Brother Daniel. I just figured the less we spoke to them the better we would be.

"Don't be ridiculous. You know she didn't have a choice," Brayley said. I rolled my eyes. "Come on. Let's finish exploring the house."

***

At midnight, the grandfather clock struck, waking me out of my sleep. It was my first night sleeping without Brayley beside me, and

I wasn't sleeping well. I turned over and stared at the small sliver of light that squeezed through the crack in the door. A knocking sound made me sit up in bed. I shivered and swung my legs over the side of the bed. I stood up and walked slowly to the door. I opened it wider revealing an empty hallway. I walked down to the next door where Brayley's bedroom was. I opened his door, and I peeked inside to see his dark figure in the bed. He was fast asleep. I closed his door softly.

I was headed back to my room when I heard the whispers. They were coming from downstairs. I walked down the staircase grazing my fingertips against the wallpaper. The whispers grew louder. They sounded like they were coming from the living area. I froze at the sound of Brother Daniel's voice.

"You're getting closer."

"I have to," the other voice said. It was Josef.

"You think she'll figure it out?" Brother Daniel asked.

"I hope not."

There was a pause.

"I want you to keep her close," Josef said.

"I don't think that's a good idea. After what I did-"

"You had to," Josef said. "She'll trust you. More than she trusts me. We need her. Alive."

"Okay."

"Just don't tell her what you did," Josef said. "But she's bound to figure out who you are."

CHAPTER 12

Once we moved in, we rarely saw our mother, and when we did, it was only for a fleeting moment. Her new position as head of the hospital kept her busy most days, and when we did see her, she was either too tired to talk or too busy to talk.

Brayley and I roamed the house like lost souls. Now that I was a Saint, my interactions with Nikki were limited to school and worship services. Brayley and I didn't have to pick corn after school anymore. Our hands healed, became soft, but our purpose was lost.

"We shouldn't be friends anymore," Nikki said one day at school. I was unsure why she would suggest such a thing because even though my family and I were Saints, we weren't welcomed among them. It was simple. My brother and I would never be invited to the table. And even if I was, there was no way I would stop being friends with Nikki.

I shook my head at her. "Why would you say that?"

"You're a Saint now."

"That's ridiculous. We're always going to be friends," I said.

"How is it anyway?"

"I hate it. I want to go back home."

Under the eye of Josef, my curiosity hadn't been satisfied. Only when I saw a small staircase at the end of the hall did something awaken in me again. I had managed to keep my curiosity at bay, and even though Josef was rarely at home, I hadn't bothered with the key. It was too risky.

One day while walking through the house I fixed my gaze on an area of the second floor that was tucked into a corner at the end of the hall. I didn't have any idea how I could've missed it, but once I noticed it, I couldn't stop looking at it. It was inevitable that I would be drawn to it.

I climbed up the small flight of steps to a small door. I expected the door to be unlocked when I turned the doorknob, but it wasn't. I examined the keyhole. It was in a familiar shape.

I dropped my hand from the door and knelt down. I pulled my dress up and reached into my boot digging my fingers inside to find the key.

"What are you doing?" a voice asked behind me.

I looked behind me to see Josef standing at the bottom of the steps. I froze and removed my fingers from the inside of my boot pretending as if I was pulling up my socks. I stood up and turned from the door.

"You didn't show us this room yet."

"I didn't think it was important."

"What is it?"

"It's the attic," Josef said flatly. "There's nothing to see."

"It's locked-"

"It's just old junk," Josef said. "Nothing important."

There was silence. He stood there as if he was waiting for me to move. It was clear he wasn't going to let me into the attic.

"Okay," I said, starting down the steps.

"Your mother wants to see you by the way," Josef said, stepping to the side as I came down the steps.

I nodded. "Thanks." I walked past him, noticing how his eyes darted to the attic door. There was something that he didn't want me to see which meant that there was something in there that I needed to see.

It was a relief when I found my mother sitting in front of her dresser mirror. I walked into their room which was identical to mine except twice as big and a slightly bigger bed. I watched as she applied powder to her cheeks in soft strokes. I noticed how my mother paid more attention to her looks. Her smell was different. Her hair was neater. And her clothes were brighter.

"Josef said you wanted to talk to me," I said.

She paused, looked at me, and then went back to powdering her face. "You scared me."

"Sorry," I said. "Going somewhere?"

"The wives of all the Elders are having a small meeting. It's just wedding stuff."

"How's that going by the way?" I asked, sitting down on their bed. It was soft like mine.

"It's fine," Mother said. "I didn't realize the big day would be so stressful."

I scoffed. "The big day?"

Mother glanced at me in the mirror's reflection. "Yes, it's a big day."

"Don't you think this is just moving a bit too fast?"

My mother paused. She stared at me in the reflection. "What do you want me to do? Make him wait?"

"Just for a little while. Just until-"

"Until nothing," Mother said, cutting me off. "October, this is happening."

"Father wouldn't have wanted this."

It was my mother's turn. She scoffed at me. "October, grow up. Your father didn't know what he wanted."

"He wanted out of here."

"Don't say that in here," she hissed at me.

I stood up. "Have fun at your little wedding party."

"I was going to invite you to come with me. All the other wives are bringing their daughters-"

"No thanks," I said, walking towards the door. I stopped at the hushed tone of her voice.

"I don't like this as much as you do," she whispered.

"Well, you sure aren't acting like it," I said without turning to look at her. She called out to me, but I ignored her and stormed out of their room.

***

That night at evening worship, I watched my mother as she conversed with the rest of the community. Josef was at her side waltzing her around as if she was some sort of door prize. I cringed at the sound of his laughter.

"October?"

I turned to Drew. "Yes?"

"You didn't hear me?" he asked.

I shook my head.

"I was asking if you were okay?" Drew asked.

"Yeah, I'm fine," I said, taking a sip from my lemonade.

"You don't seem fine," Drew said.

"What?" I looked back at him. He raised an eyebrow. "Oh, I'm sorry. I have a lot on my mind."

"You want to talk about it?"

I sighed. "I don't know what's worse. My father's disappearance or this."

Drew glanced at my mother. "Your mother's doing a really good job at faking it."

"That's the problem," I murmured. "I don't think she is."

"Maybe it's a good thing," Drew said.

"How?"

"Think of it this way," Drew said. "You're getting closer to his secrets."

He had a point.

Something caught my attention over Drew's shoulder. It was Ward. He was walking near the stage. I took Drew's hand.

"I'll be back," I said to Drew and squeezed his hand.

"Where are you going?" Drew asked, but I was already walking off and headed into Ward's direction.

"Brother Ward!" I called out to him. Ward stopped and turned to look at me. I caught up to him, noticing the way he stared at me. "Hi."

"Hi," Ward said.

He stared at me with an intensity that almost made me stumble for my words.

"It's been awhile," I said.

"Yeah," Ward said. "How've you been?"

"Alright, I guess."

Ward narrowed his eyes at me. "I thought living with our dear prophet would be like paradise."

I laughed. "Yeah, not so much."

Ward shoved his hands into his pockets. "I was gonna say hi, but you were a little busy."

"Oh," I blushed. I looked over my shoulder to see that Drew was still standing by the drinks. Zan had joined him. I turned back to Ward. "I have something to tell you."

Ward furrowed his eyebrows. I glanced around to see that no one was paying attention to us, but I wanted to be careful. I grabbed Ward by the wrist. He stiffened underneath my grip. I pulled him behind the stage.

"Everything okay?" he asked, looking down at my hand on his wrist.

"Josef has an attic in his house."

Ward raised an eyebrow. "And?" He wasn't getting where I was going.

"The attic was locked," I said to him. "I was going to open it, but Josef stopped me."

"How were you going to open it if it was locked?" Ward asked.

Ward didn't know that I had the key. "That's not the point." He raised an eyebrow at me. "The point is that Josef didn't want me in the attic. He wouldn't tell me what was in there either."

"Soooo…" Ward shook his head. "I'm still not getting it."

"It means we need to find out what's in that attic. It might have something to do with my father's disappearance."

CHAPTER 13

The wedding seemed to come earlier than I wanted it to. It all happened so fast. One minute we were moving into his house and the next, we were setting up the house for the wedding. It was happening. The permanent link between him and us would be tied with a matrimonial knot.

It was the day of the wedding and the house was bustling with activity. There were people everywhere. Sister Celine led some of the women in the kitchen as they cooked, baked, and shaped the wedding food. The men were led by Brother Daniel who barked orders as they decorated the backyard. My mother was nowhere in sight as I imagined her room was preoccupied with the other women helping her dress, fixing her hair, and dollying her up.

I was walking past the kitchen on my way up the stairs to get ready when a sweet aroma wafted up my nose. I inhaled deeply and moaned at the delicious smell.

"You're drooling," a voice said behind me.

I turned to see that Genevieve was standing at the front door with a tall bag slung across her shoulder. "Genevieve?"

"Don't look so happy," she said.

"Why are you here?"

"I'm in the wedding."

There was a pause as we stared at each other. I finally turned back to the stairs and started walking up them. "You can use my room to get dressed."

"Thanks." She followed me to my room. When she stepped inside, she looked around. "Nice," she smirked.

"The bathroom's right th-" Genevieve headed in the direction of the bathroom before I could finish my sentence. "How do you know-" She shut the bathroom door, cutting me off just as a knock sounded on my bedroom door. It was Josef. He was dressed in his white buttoned down shirt and black slacks.

"Did Genevieve make it?" he asked, rolling up his sleeves.

"Yeah, she's getting dressed."

"Okay, people will start arriving soon. Just wanted to make sure you'll be ready in time."

"I will."

"This is a special day, October. I hope you're happy with all of this. Your mother sure is," Josef said with a small smile.

I opened my mouth to retort when suddenly the bathroom door opened and Genevieve stepped out.

"Hey October, the-" she froze at the sight of Josef.

Josef looked her over. His eyes trailing down her body. Genevieve blushed and looked down at the ground.

"You look beautiful, Genevieve," Josef said softly.

"Thank you, uncle," she mumbled.

Watching the two of them was enlightening. Genevieve shrinked underneath Josef's eye, and for the first time, I saw her weakness. The very thing that made Genevieve just as vulnerable as the rest of us.

Josef cleared his throat directing my attention back to him. "Well, I'll be seeing you ladies in a few." He nodded curtly at us and then left.

I turned to Genevieve. She looked up at me, and the vulnerability was replaced with anger or rather she was using the anger to hide what she was really feeling.

"You should hurry and dress," she said, curtly walking out of my room. "This wedding is happening with or without you."

***

A couple of hours later, I found myself at the front door greeting guests. I tugged at the long collar on my pastel dress.

"Stop worrying," Brayley said. "You look pretty."

I smiled. "You look handsome yourself."

He smiled at me. Suddenly, a familiar face crossed the threshold.

"Hi," Drew said, walking into the house.

"Hi."

"You look beautiful," Drew said, eyeing me. His lips curled in the corners. I bit my lip to hide how thrilled I was to see him.

"You look good too," I said. Drew was dressed in a dark button shirt and light pants. The dark shirt contrasted with his hair and eyes making them look brighter. As I stared at him, I was suddenly aware of the desire to rub my fingers through his hair.

"Drew!" Genevieve's shrill voice startled me, making me jump. We all looked towards the staircase to see her coming down. I rolled my eyes. Somehow she managed to make herself look ten times better than me even though we were wearing the same thing.

"Hey, Genevieve," Drew said, glancing back and forth between the two of us. "You guys should match more often."

I shot him a look. He laughed.

The ceremony started as soon as all the guests were seated. As soon as the music began, Genevieve and I walked together down the aisle carrying a bouquet of white roses. I looked over at the crowd as they smiled at us. After we made our way down the aisle, it was Brayley's turn. He carried a pillow that held two rings on them: one for Mother and one for Josef. He walked to the other side of the altar and stood there staring at the crowd. He looked terrified, so I caught his eye and winked at him. He managed a smile.

Suddenly, everyone stood up. I watched as Josef came down the aisle grinning from ear to ear. He acknowledged the crowd on the way to the altar. He stood in front of Brayley and straightened his tie. He caught me staring and pursed his lips together. I had never seen him look so nervous.

The crowd gasped. I looked down the aisle to see my mother. Her skin glowed, and her eyes sparkled. Her hair spilled down her shoulders in waves. Her dress was white and lacy, and it bellowed out underneath her in a silhouette that made her look like a queen.

Tears swelled in my eyes, and I wiped them away quickly on the back of my hand. I didn't know why I was crying. I just knew that my mother was breathtaking. As she made her way down the aisle, her eyes found mine. I hadn't seen her this happy in a long time.

Josef held his hand out for her to take as she neared the altar. She grabbed his hand and stepped in front of him. The crowd sat down.

Josef cleared his throat. "Today is a very special day for us. Today I get to marry you." The crowd awed. "Lauren from the first day I laid eyes on you I knew we were meant to be together. I promise to never leave you, and I promise to protect you."

My mother smiled. "I love you Josef, and I can't wait to be your wife."

Josef beckoned for Brayley to step forward. Brayley held out the pillow, and they grabbed the rings. He grabbed Mother's left hand. "With this ring I thee wed." He slid the ring on her finger.

My mother grabbed Josef's left hand. "With this ring I thee wed." She slid the ring on his finger.

"I pronounce us husband and wife," Josef said.

I drew in a sharp breath. I watched as Josef's dark eyes raked over her body. He bent down and kissed her. Their union was sealed. The crowd erupted in applause.

I could remember watching them from the hallway as they danced in the living room. My mother's head was laid across my father's chest. Her hands in his as they swayed to whatever invisible music they were listening to.

He spun her around, and she chuckled. Her laughter was soft. He pulled her close to him, wrapping his hand around her waist.

"You've always been a good dancer," my mother had said. She laid her head back on his chest and closed her eyes. "Do you remember our wedding?"

"Of course," my father had said. "It was one of the happiest days of my life."

She looked up at him and he bent down to kiss her softly.

"Would you like to dance?" a voice woke me from my daze.

I stood by the sidelines watching the crowd. Some danced. Some talked. My mother and Josef were being congratulated. Brayley was in the patio area with Nadia. They grinned and talked as if nothing else mattered to them. I spotted Nikki by the refreshments near Zan.

I looked at Drew who was standing beside me. "I'm not a good dancer."

"I don't care," Drew said, holding his hand out to me. I smiled and took it.

Drew pulled me to him, laying the other hand on my waist. My breath quickened with the racing of my heart. I followed Drew's lead.

"You're a good dancer."

"Thanks," he said. "How are you feeling about all of this?"

I shook my head. "I knew it was going to happen. I just didn't think it really would. Everything about this wedding is just wrong."

"I know," Drew said.

"And you know what's worse?" I asked him. "Everyone else seems to think it's okay." I looked up at him as he stared at me intensely.

"Maybe it will be," Drew said.

His mouth was inches away. He reached down, moving his lips closer to mine. I wanted to reach up to kiss him, but instead I laid my head on his chest.

"We can't."

There was silence as we swayed to the music for a while. The feel of him underneath me soothed me. I caught a glimpse of the back door that led into the house, and I saw Brother Daniel standing by it. I waited a few seconds. He finally walked away from the door. This was my chance.

I lifted my head up. Drew stared down at me.

"What's wrong?" he asked.

"I have an idea."

"What is it?"

"The attic," I said. "While Josef is distracted, I can see what he's hiding in there."

"What if he sees us?" Drew asked.

"He won't," I said, grabbing his hand. "Come on." I pulled him through the crowd making my way to the back door.

"October?" another voice called over to me. This time I stopped. I glanced over to see that it was Ward. He walked up to me. He looked handsome, but I couldn't think about that right now.

"You look like you're in a rush," he said. His eyes darted over to Drew.

"I am. Follow me," I said to him. Ward nodded and followed me to the back door. I placed my hand on the doorknob.

"What are you doing?" a voice asked behind us.

I dropped my hand from the door and spun around. It was Brother Daniel.

"Um-" I stammered trying to come up with a lie.

"We're helping with refreshments," Drew interrupted. I heaved a sigh of relief. "We're just bringing out some more food."

Brother Daniel narrowed his eyes at us. He waited a few seconds before responding, "I know what you're doing. Go and hurry."

"How do you-"

"Go!" Brother Daniel barked. "He doesn't have much time!"

"'He?'" I was confused.

"October, let's go!" Ward said, opening the door. I ran inside following him with Drew close behind.

"Wait," Drew said once the door was closed. He looked back and forth between Ward and I. "What's going on?"

I walked up to him, grabbing his hand. "Drew, I promise I'll explain later, but right now you have to trust me. We need to get to the attic."

He nodded hesitantly.

I smiled. I wanted to explain, but now was not the time. "Let's go."

We hurried out of the kitchen and dashed up the staircase. I raced up the small steps that led up to the attic door and took out my key from my boot.

"It was you this whole time, huh?" Ward shook his head, staring at the key. He snorted. "I should've known."

I unlocked the door. It creaked open, and I stepped inside. The attic was large and spacious. I looked over at the wall to see that the window had been boarded up. Light peeked in through the slits between the boards, but it wasn't enough to light the room. Ward went over to the window and attempted to remove one of the boards so that we could get more light.

I put my hand out in front of me and started moving deeper inside. I moved around piles of boxes and old furniture.

"What are we looking for?" Drew asked.

"I don't know," I said. "But Josef's hiding something."

"Like what?" Ward asked, yanking at the bottom board.

"Brother Daniel said something about a 'he.'"

"Who's 'he?'" Drew asked.

"I don't know-"

That's when I heard it. The moaning wasn't audible at first. It wasn't until I tilted my head could I hear it. It was a low groan.

"I hear something," I said.

Drew shook his head. "I don't hear anything."

"Shhh!" I moved in the direction of the noise as the others went quiet. There was no mistaking it this time. The moan was coming from the back of the attic. I moved slowly, careful not to knock into anything. My breath quickened. Suddenly, it came into focus. A dark shape. I approached the dark shape that was in the corner of the attic.

I couldn't believe what I was seeing. It was like the hand of God had reached out and turned on a light switch. It felt like a dream, but even dreams that seemed impossible to imagine were just miracles waiting to happen. In the dim light of the attic that miracle had happened.

In tattered filthy clothes was my father. His foot was chained to a spot just below a dirty mattress and an empty bowl that was probably where he had his food and water. My father lifted up his head slowly. His face was dirty with a beard and shaggy hair that came down to his chest. When he looked at me, I could no longer hear I could no longer think. "You're alive?" is all I could manage to get out before I dropped to my knees.

I collapsed at the sound of my father calling out my name.

WINTER

CHAPTER 14

It was a cold, heavy winter for Blue Corn. It was like the snow had become a permanent blanket for the ground. It covered the houses, it covered the trees, and it covered the corn. When the snow got too thick, Sister Jennifer was ordered by Josef to close the schoolhouse until the snow lightened. I was relieved that we didn't have school, but that meant we were forced to stay around the house more. That meant I couldn't visit my father as often as I wanted to.

I didn't remember much after we had found him, only what Drew told me. He told me that I had collapsed at the sight of my father. Drew had to carry me back to my room while Ward snuck my father out of the attic. That next morning I had woken up with a tiny note on the dresser telling me to meet the others at the Keegan's shop. I would be told the rest then.

Ward met us at the shop along with Nikki. It turned out she kept an eye on me while Drew and Ward snuck my father out of the house. They had put him in the old barn. It was now late winter, and I worried about him. The farmers used the barn sometimes, but Ward promised he would keep them away from where my father was hiding. I was more worried about the cold. Even though he was inside and we had given him plenty of blankets, it was freezing at night. I didn't know how much longer we could keep him hidden.

"I'm sorry," my father said to me one afternoon. I would go visit him to bring him some of our leftovers. It wasn't much, but he was happy to have it.

I never thought I would know what happened that day he disappeared. I figured it was something he had seen. Maybe he had been a witness to some sort of forbidden act that Josef hadn't wanted him to know about. It would've made sense. The truth was that it was simple. My father had tried to leave and was caught before he had gotten the chance to escape.

"Why would you leave us?" I asked him, looking over the railing down at the barn floor. My father was hiding on the second floor of the barn. The ladder leading up to the second floor was thin and threatening to break at every move, but somehow it was still holding on.

"I wasn't going to leave you. I would've come back, October," my father said, coming to stand beside me.

I shook my head. "After all this time, I thought you were taken from us."

"I was," he said.

"You left," I said. "Without telling us."

"It wasn't like that," he said. "I was there at the fence and I figured I should at least try it. Maybe I could. I thought I could. I was going to come back for you. October, I was going to get help."

"Without me?" I asked. "Without us?" This felt like the biggest betrayal. Even more than the wedding.

"I'm sorry," my father said, placing a hand on my shoulder. I shrugged it off. "I don't know what else to say."

"Would you leave us if you had the chance?" I had asked him one day. He was helping out in the cornfields filling my bucket with kernels of corn. He could pick faster than I could and had already filled a bucket and was working on the second one.

"No," I remembered my father saying.

"Why not?" I had asked. "You would have your freedom. That's what you want, right?"

"Freedom doesn't mean anything if I don't have my family by my side," my father had said looking at me. I smiled. My father smiled back.

"Good," I said.

"It's fine," I said, sniffing away the tears. "You're okay now. That's all that matters."

There was silence. The tension between us was heartbreaking. I hadn't expected this type of response from him.

"You okay?"

"I'll see you later," I said, looking back at his makeshift bed.

"Thank you for the food," he said.

"The crops are dying. It's hardly anything."

The winter was particularly harsh. It brought disaster and ruin for us. I overheard in some of the Elder's meetings how the farm was underperforming. Josef always boasted that our community was untouchable but that winter, snow had frozen the bushels and covered the fields. We couldn't produce enough corn because the crops were dying, and if we didn't have the money from the corn, then we couldn't buy what we needed to sustain our community. Everyone was living on edge being that our supplies were draining fast.

The effects of the dying crops showed in the faces of the Sinners. Nikki's face had sunken in, and her dress had begun to hang loosely over her shoulders. Like with my father, I snuck food for her. During church. During worship. Bread. A small bag of vegetables. Cookies from Drew. I would've snuck more, but Josef had forbidden us to help them. He had said that this was part of their punishment. They hadn't worked hard enough to keep the crops from dying so this was what they deserved. It was disgusting to hear him tell us things like that. If it was anyone's fault, it was his.

One day we were seated around the fire that Brother Daniel made us. My mother was boiling water for tea and soup, and Josef had said it once again. I had had enough and I finally said something in response, "Maybe this is your punishment." He hadn't responded back. I wasn't sure if he had heard me, but he had clenched his jaw when I said it which meant he had.

"It's more than enough," my father said, bringing my attention back to him.

I nodded. I gave him a small smile before starting down the ladder. When I got to the bottom, I jumped down onto the ground. I dusted myself off pulling my hood over my head. I could feel my father's eyes on my back watching me, but I didn't turn around. I opened the barn door and stepped out into the cold afternoon air. The road was empty.

I didn't have any intentions on going there, but somehow I ended up at the Keegan's shop. The other shops had big CLOSED signs covering the windows on their doors. I spotted Drew standing at the door to his family's shop. He was locking the door.

"Hey, what are you doing?" I asked, walking up to him.

He turned to look at me then turned back to the door pulling on the lock to make sure it was secure.

"Closing up shop," he said.

"Why?" I asked.

"We don't have anything to sell," Drew said, turning back to me.

"Is there anything I can do to help?"

"No," Drew said. "Until the crops come back, we're all screwed."

He stepped towards me, closing the space between us. I didn't move. The wedding day had been so hectic I had forgotten that something had changed between Drew and I. We hadn't had the chance to talk about it. But now we could.

Drew took my hand making the heat rise in my chest. "How's your father?" he asked.

"Fine," I said. "The barn was the perfect spot. Josef hasn't suspected a thing yet."

"Good," he said, staring into my eyes. I bit my lip to hide my smile. "We never got a chance to talk about what happened at the wedding."

"What happened?" I asked.

Drew glanced around to make sure no one was around. He pulled me to the side of the shop. I pressed myself against the wooden building staring up at him. He placed his other hand on my waist, drawing circles on it with his fingers.

"I want to talk about us," Drew said.

I smiled up at him. "What about us?"

"This," he said, squeezing my hand and pulling me closer to him. I stood up on my tiptoes and brushed my nose against his. It was cold, but I liked it. He kissed me. His soft lips clung to mine at first then moved with more urgency. He tasted like chocolate. I sighed against his lips and murmured his name. My hands moved into his hair, and he kissed me harder. I felt like I was on fire.

We pulled apart for a moment breathing cold air into each other's face. He smiled down at me.

"I've been wanting to do that since the wedding," he said breathlessly.

I smiled back because I had been wanting the same thing.

CHAPTER 15

Drew and I began to meet everyday. Whenever we could. Wherever we could. Even though the weather was cold, our obsession with each other was hot. In the cornfields. In the woods near the frozen pond. We even snuck back inside of his family shop. We couldn't get enough of each other, and even after our conversation went dull, just the feel of his presence was enough to fill the silence between us.

"Have you asked for forgiveness yet?" Drew asked me one night as we laid together on a makeshift pallet he had made us on the floor of the shop. Candles surrounded us and flickering light played across his face as I could see him watching me.

I held his hand drawing circles on the inside of his palms. "For what?"

"For us?" he asked. "What we're doing. It's-"

"I'm not sorry for anything," I told him. Our attraction to each other had grown each day. At first his touch had been enough but then I had wanted more. His kisses had sustained me for a while. Finally, I couldn't deny what I had been feeling, and our bodies had become one. Melting into each other was like heaven. The warmth of him filled me in a different way than I could have ever imagined.

He smiled and kissed my nose. And just like that he didn't ask anything else about it. We enjoyed each other regardless of what anyone thought about it.

Neither my mother nor Brayley questioned my whereabouts. I wasn't sure if it was because they didn't know that I had been leaving or they just didn't care to ask. We sat at dinner some nights alone without Josef. Ever since the winter had brought the death of the cornfields, Josef had been distant. He was rarely at home, and when he was, he was always in his study with the door closed. I would ask my mother what kept him away and she would simply say that he was busy dealing with the farm. Our community would only survive if the farm survived and with the dying of the crops, our survival had been threatened.

"What if this place finally goes down?" I asked her.

"October, don't talk like that," my mother said.

"You still want it to, right?" I asked. "Because I do."

"October…" Mother said, giving me a warning glance.

"I don't want the crops to die," Brayley said. "I don't want to die."

"You're not going to die," I said firmly.

My mother stood up abruptly from the table. Her soup slushed against the sides of her bowl. "I can't talk about this right now."

"Why?"

She pinched the bridge of her nose. "October, I'm tired. Josef has been working really hard and I don't want to hear your complaints. Nothing's going to change."

"Fine. Go to your room," I said. "It's what you've been doing anyway."

My mother scoffed. "What does that supposed to mean?"

"Nothing," I said. She narrowed her eyes at me and said nothing. She shook her head at me disappointingly before leaving. I looked at Brayley who was shaking his head in a disapproving manner. "What?"

"You didn't have to say all that," he said.

I shrugged. "It's the truth."

"Still," Brayley said.

"When was the last time you had an honest conversation with her?" I asked him.

Brayley shrugged. "I don't know."

"Okay then."

"You too," he said.

"What does that supposed to mean?"

"You're always gone. You don't think we notice? You're never home and when you are home you're getting ready to leave. What's going on?" Brayley asked.

I froze. I hadn't told them that I had found my father. I couldn't trust my mother anymore, but I could trust Brayley. I just didn't know how he would react.

"Nothing's going on," I lied. "I've just been spending a lot of time with Drew."

"Drew?" Brayley asked. "Are you two…"

"We're together, yes."

"You can't do that."

"When have I ever listened?" I asked, getting up from the table.

"Where are you going now?" he asked incredulously.

"I'm going to go apologize to Mother," I said, rolling my eyes.

"You should," he said, shoving soup into his mouth.

I walked out of the dining area and headed up the staircase to their bedroom. I could see that the door was ajar when I got up to the top of the stairs, but instead of going inside, I waited. I could see her sitting on the bed near the nightstand. She pulled open the top dresser on the nightstand and pulled out a bottle of white pills. The same pills I had seen when we lived back in our cottage. She opened the bottle and poured some of the pills into the palm of her hand. She tilted her head back and placed the pills in her mouth, swallowing them. I watched as she put the bottle back into the nightstand and laid down.

At that moment it seemed to me that an apology wouldn't have made anything better. I was struck by her strange sense of coping. It was different for everyone. The way I coped was loud and outspoken like the thunderous clap in a storm. Hers was quiet. A sort of numbness that carried her. I wondered if telling her about my father would make her feel better. I began to doubt that she felt anything at all.

I backed away not wanting to interrupt her. I turned and walked slowly back down the stairs. I paused at the bottom of the stairs and sat down.

A thud sounded to the right of me. I stood and looked over to where Josef's study was. A sliver of light peeked from underneath the door. I could see black shadows moving across the bottom of the door indicating that someone was walking around.

I stepped down from the stairs and walked over to the study door. Another streak of light squeezed through the keyhole. I knelt down and aligned my eye to its opening.

Inside I could see that Josef wasn't alone. I didn't know he was having an Elder's meeting. They must have snuck in through the back door while we were eating.

I could see that the Elders were kneeled on the ground in what appeared to be a circle. They all looked up at Josef who was standing in the middle of the circle. His back was to me, but I could see that he was holding his arms out in front of him.

"We praise her," I could hear Josef's muffled voice say.

He turned and in one hand he was holding a knife. He held it to his wrist. I gasped and held my hand over my mouth to cover the sound. Zan's father, Brother Alex, held a jar in front of Josef. Josef cut just above his wrist with the knife and squeezed blood into the jar that Brother Alex held out for him.

I backed away from the keyhole and inhaled a shaky breath. I was confused. What was Josef doing? And why had he said 'her' instead of Him. Who was he giving his blood too?

"Have you seen his god?" I would ask my father. He would take me to the pond when we were tired of the house. Tired of the farm. Tired of it all and we just needed to get away.

My father looked up at me from staring down into the water. His eyes were deep. "No," I could remember his answer because I thought he would have said something different. The honesty between my father and I was the realest thing we had. "No one has."

"What are you doing?" a voice whispered to the side of me. I looked to see that Brother Daniel was standing in the foyer watching me.

"I, um-" I stumbled for the right words to say because I didn't know how to tell him that I had just caught Josef in some sort of blood ritual.

Brother Daniel started to walk towards me, and I got up from the floor. I was frozen in place.

"He's in a meeting," Brother Daniel said, walking up to me.

"I know," I said. I didn't know if Brother Daniel had seen the look of terror on my face, but the way he pulled me to the side must have meant that he had.

"What did you see?" he whispered to me after pulling me back near the staircase. Before the wedding, Brother Daniel had been distant but ever since that day at the wedding he had been different. He had known that my father was in the attic, and he didn't stop me from finding him. In fact, on that day it seemed like he wanted me to find him. I still didn't know who he was, but the mere action of not stopping me had shown me that maybe I could trust him.

"What is he doing?"

Brother Daniel sighed. He looked up at the ceiling and closed his eyes. "You weren't supposed to see that."

"What is he doing?" I repeated myself. My voice shook.

"He's just trying to help," Brother Daniel said. "October, our crops are dying. Our community is not going to make it long without food."

"What does that have to do with anything?" I asked, hinting to the study.

Brother Daniel pinched the bridge of his nose. "It's not about the crops, October."

"What does that mean?" I asked him. He shook his head. "Why did he say 'her?' Who's 'her?' What's going on?"

"I can't say," he said to me. "Just act normal, okay?"

"I'm supposed to act like I didn't just see him do that?"

"Yes, please," he pleaded. "Brother Josef can not know that you saw him. No one is supposed to know besides the Elders. I'm not even supposed to know."

I gawked at him. "Know what?"

Brother Daniel shook his head. "I can't say."

"Just answer me one question then," I said to him. He stared at me waiting. "We're not worshipping God, are we?"

Brother Daniel pursed his lips. Finally, he shook his head. "No. Not at all."

CHAPTER 16

The news traveled fast. Sister Abigail had been found dead in the cornfields. Sister Abigail had a daughter Hannah. I remembered Hannah from the cornfields. She was so frail. Her mother had that same sense of frailness too. Always just a bit too skinny. Skin just off color. Bones protruding from the wrist that extended into bony fingers. I didn't know if the rumors were true, but we all heard that when they found her body her eyes had been scratched out. Her skin had taken on a pale grayish color, and she had gotten so skinny that her body had shriveled in the snow almost making it hard for them to see her. But they had found her. A trail of blood had led them to her body, and when they saw her frozen shape, the blood that had dripped from her eyes down into the snow had frozen into tiny red icicles that dangled off her face.

Her death sparked even more panic and rage among us. The cornfields were still dying and even the people who had lived comfortably had noticed the dwindling of their food supply. It was evident in church that Sunday. After Josef's sermon, which was particularly short, someone had asked about Sister Abigail's death and whether it was a suspected murder or suicide.

"Sister Abigail's death was unfortunate. She will be missed, but this wasn't a murder," Josef explained to us. We all stared at him. Some people took his word, but I could see that others had skeptical looks on their faces. This was the first time that I saw so many people who weren't in agreement with him.

"Why was she in the cornfields?" a voice blurted out from the back of the crowd. "What was she trying to do?"

"We don't know," Josef said, holding his hand out to silence the noise. "All we know is that she froze to death."

"What are we going to do about the cornfields?" Brother Jack asked. "Some of us are starving and some of us are starting to feel hungry. It's not going to be long before something worse happens."

"I understand," Josef said, nodding. "But the Elders and I-"

"Are doing what exactly?" I asked, interrupting him. I stood up. Josef's face turned red. There was silence as he stared at me blankly. I could hear my mother sigh underneath her breath. "We need real help."

The crowd went silent.

"I think October's right," a voice behind me said. I turned to see that it was Zan. His family was seated a couple of pews behind us. He looked at me and nodded. He turned his attention back to Josef.

"What if we sent someone to the outside? A couple people can get enough food to last us through the winter-"

"No," Josef said quietly.

"Zan's right," I said. "It can be a one time thing-"

"No!" Josef's voice boomed through the church. It silenced us. "Have we lost our purpose just because we're hungry? Have we forgotten that the outside is evil and that our heaven is here? Why would we risk that for food?" Josef looked us over. Some people in the crowd held their heads down in shame. "There will be no contact with the outside. It's not our way," Josef turned his attention to me. "We will not turn our back on everything we've built just to satisfy some earthly desire. We pray and we wait for winter to be over."

"We'll all die by then," I muttered.

"October, sit down," my mother mumbled under her breath.

"We will-" Josef started.

"We're all going to die by then," I said, interrupting him again. This time louder.

Everyone stared at me. Not because of what I had said but because of my refusal to take Josef's word for what it was.

"Come," Josef said to me. I expected him to be angry with me, but he was calm. I hesitated. He held his arms out beckoning for me to come to the front. I could hear my mother muttering for me to go. So I did. I walked to the front of the church and stood next to Josef. He placed both of his hands on my shoulders. I didn't know if the others could see it, but Josef tightened his grip. "Our community was founded to keep us safe," Josef said to the crowd. "When the time comes, we will join our Lord in paradise, but for now, our work is here. To stay here. To continue to build this community. Our time will come. Annual Harvest is upon us."

The crowd began to nod in agreement. They started to repeat after him.

"Annual Harvest is upon us," I heard their voices in the crowd begin to recite. They looked at us in reverence as Josef's grip on my shoulders tightened even more. I winced. "ANNUAL HARVEST IS UPON US!"

I looked over to where Nikki was sitting. Her eyes were wide. She looked frightened. She shook her head at me. My protest was over. They had just accepted their fate.

***

"You're right, you know?" a voice said to me that night at worship. I stood at the sidelines watching Josef. He was talking to Brother Daniel. Brother Daniel glanced over at me, and I turned my attention away from them. I looked beside me to see Zan.

"Oh yeah?" I asked.

"Yeah," Zan said. "The crops are dying. Supplies are low. It's like he doesn't care."

"He doesn't," I mumbled and crossed my arms against my chest.

"What do you think we should do-"

"What do you want Zan?" I asked, cutting him off. I could count with one hand the number of times Zan and I had spoken to each other, and there had never been a pleasant interaction between the two of us. I didn't understand why he had come to talk to me now. "We aren't friends."

Zan opened his mouth to object then decided against it. "I know," he sighed. "Look, I'm sorry, October. I was never nice to you or Nikki. I was just being a Saint."

"You were being an ass."

Zan pursed his lips. He nodded. "You're right and I shouldn't have acted that way. I know it doesn't seem like it, but I think you're brave." I raised an eyebrow at him questioningly. "I see why Drew wants to be around you." Zan smiled. "You're real."

I stared at him. I didn't understand where all this was coming from. I felt a touch on my hand, and I looked behind me to see that Nikki was staring at us. Her mouth hung slightly open as she stared at Zan. Luckily, he couldn't see the flush of her cheeks underneath the glow of the bonfire.

"Hi," Zan said to her.

"Hi," Nikki said shyly.

They stared at each other for a few more seconds before Nikki averted her gaze.

"What's going on here?" Drew asked, walking up to us.

"We're just chatting," Zan said, patting Drew on the back. He smiled slyly. "October and I just came to an understanding."

I snorted. "I almost forgot about that. Drew, meet our new best friend."

Drew laughed. "So you and Zan are good?"

"For now," I said, watching as Zan's attention fell back on Nikki.

"Well, good," Drew said. "I thought I would have to cut you off Zan. We run a tight ship around here."

Zan was too busy staring at Nikki to respond. "Would you like to dance with me?" he asked her.

"Dance?" Nikki asked. She looked around as if to see if he was really talking to her. "With me? Can you?"

"I can do whatever I want," Zan said. He extended his hand. Nikki looked to me as if to ask for permission. I raised an eyebrow and shrugged. She took it, and Zan led her away from us. Drew and I watched as he led her near the bonfire. He whispered something into her ear, and she laughed.

"Well…" I said, watching as Zan placed his hand on Nikki's lower back. "That happened fast."

Drew laughed. We watched them for a few seconds before I broke the silence.

"I saw something."

"Saw what?"

I glanced around to see if someone was watching us before continuing, "Josef was cutting himself."

"What?" Drew asked incredulously. "What are you talking about?"

"Him and the Elders. I saw them. They were making themselves bleed in a jar."

"Why?"

"I don't know," I said, shaking my head. I looked over at the crowd. Josef was talking to some of the Elders. I looked down at his wrist to see that his sleeves were rolled up. He glanced over at me unconsciously pulling the sleeves down over his wrist. "But I think they're feeding something."

CHAPTER 17

A small kinky-haired girl with blood splattered across her dress grinned into the mirror with blood stained teeth. Her smile was wide. Too wide. She held a long pitchfork in her hands.

The little girl moved her tongue against the front of her teeth, wiping off the remnants of blood. She moved the pitchfork into the crevices of her shoulder. The front end of the pitchfork pointed against the mirror at her reflection. She closed one eye. The other stared into the mirror.

Suddenly, a clawed hand placed itself on the girl's shoulder. The hand was grayish and wrinkled. Its nails were long and ragged.

"Praise me," a woman's voice whispered.

The girl smiled into the mirror for a split second more and then jabbed the pitchfork into the mirror shattering the reflection.

I woke up to the sound of breaking glass.

"October?" a voice called out to me.

I looked around my room. Moonlight from the sky streamed in through my curtains making shadows that danced across my room.

"October?" Brayley called out to me. I looked at Brayley who was standing in my doorway. He stared at me with wide eyes. "You were having a bad dream. You were screaming."

"I, what?" I asked, pulling my covers up to my chin.

"What were you dreaming about?" he asked.

"Nothing," I said. That girl standing in the mirror hadn't been some stranger. It had been me. I didn't know what it meant. But I didn't have a good feeling about it.

"Can I sleep with you?" he asked.

"Yeah," I said, moving back the covers and scooting over to make space for him. "What's wrong?"

"It's Mother," he said, climbing into bed beside me.

"What about her?" I asked.

Brayley looked down into the palms of his hands where he was twiddling his thumbs. "I think something's wrong with her. I listen to them sometimes. Mother and Brother Josef..."

"What do they say?"

"Something about pills," he said. "She takes a lot of them. She's making him get them for her. I'm scared, October. What if something happens to her?"

"Hey," I said, putting my arms around his shoulder. "It's okay. Nothing's going to happen to her."

Brayley leaned his head against my shoulder. "I don't want her to die, October."

"Brayley, she's not going to die," I said to him, rubbing his back. He began to cry. "She's not going to die."

***

"Tell them what you saw," Drew urged me.

Nikki and Zan stared at me blankly. We all had agreed to meet inside Drew's father's shop. It was the only place we could get together without looking too suspicious. It was the only place where we were free to talk. Drew had brought Zan along. It seemed as if Zan had become to us what Drew once was. A stranger turned ally. Turned lover for some. Zan sat beside Nikki, and even though I couldn't see it, I could tell that they were holding hands underneath the table.

"I don't want you to be scared," I said to them, particularly to Nikki. "But I saw something."

"What did you see?" she asked.

Suddenly, the door opened to the shop, and Ward stepped in tracking in snow under his boots.

"What is he doing here?" Drew whispered to me.

"I asked him to come," I said.

Drew furrowed his eyebrows, confused. "Why?"

I ignored him and got up from the table. I walked over to Ward. He was shivering slightly. Snow covered the collar of his jacket and on the hat he was wearing. His long hair peeped out from underneath.

"You made it," I said.

Ward nodded once. "You sure they want me here?"

"Yes," I said. "We need you...I need you."

Ward nodded. I looked back at the others. Drew stared at Ward in quiet reproach.

"What is he doing here?" Zan asked. Ward narrowed his eyes at Zan.

"Ward is a heretic. Just like us. He feels the same way. About this place. About Josef. He can help," I said.

"Help us do what exactly?" Zan asked.

"Escape," I said.

There was silence as they all stared at me. We had all talked about it. Wanted it. But no one had ever said it. My father had tried and failed. But this time, it would be different. I wanted it to be different, and this time we wouldn't leave anyone behind.

"How are we going to pull that off?" Zan asked. "You have a plan?"

"No," I said. "But we have each other and that's all we need."

"October, you saw what happened to your father when he tried to get out of here," Nikki said. "Josef isn't going to let us leave."

"We're starving, Nikki," I said. "And that's not the worst part. There's something wrong with this place, and we need to get out of here before it's too late."

"You didn't tell them," Drew said, shaking his head. "The Elders…"

Zan sat up. "What about the Elders?"

"They were cutting themselves," I said. "It was like some kind of ritual. They were collecting their blood in a jar like they were giving it to someone."

"What?" Zan asked in disbelief. "You're lying."

"No," I said. "Look at your dad's wrist. You'll see the marks."

Nikki shuddered. "We can't stay here. We have to go."

I nodded in agreement. "I need us together on this." I looked at Ward who looked doubtful. "Please."

"I'm in," Zan said. "Come on. We all know this place isn't right."

I looked back at Ward. He was reluctant, but he nodded. "Alright, I'm in. Whatever it takes."

I heaved a sigh of relief. That's what I needed to hear.

Drew looked down at his watch. "We should go. It's time for worship."

Although we usually held worship outside in the church's backyard, we now held them in the church because it was too cold. On the way to the church, Drew nudged me with his shoulder. He was walking closer to me than the others. I looked at him to see that he had a worried look on his face.

"How do you know you can trust him?" Drew whispered to me. He was hinting to Ward who was walking further away from the group.

"I just do," I said to him. "Trust me, okay?"

Drew nodded. He moved his hand over to mine taking it into his hand. I squeezed his hand in reassurance. Once we got to the church, Drew released his hand from mine. I looked over at Nikki and Zan, and they weren't standing as close to each other. I looked back to see that Ward had disappeared.

We walked into the church, and it was already full. I realized that we were the last ones to arrive. There was a quiet hush among the others. Some of them avoided our gaze. Some stared down into the palms of their twitchy fingers. Others looked at us and shook their heads disapprovingly.

"Something's wrong," Drew whispered.

I froze when I saw the small smirk on Genevieve's face. "What's going on?" I was reluctant to take another step.

There was no answer. My mother started to sob. I looked at Brayley, and his eyes went wide. He was trying to tell me something.

Suddenly, Josef came out of his office rolling up his sleeves.

I took a step back. "What's going on?"

"I told you uncle!" Genevieve yelled. She stood up and pointed her fingers at us. "I told you. They're together!"

"What?" I asked.

"You and Drew. Nikki and Zan. You're together. That's against the rules," Genevieve said.

"What are you talking about?" I asked, holding my hands up in defense.

"I know what you four have been doing," Josef said.

"Brother Josef, what do you mean?" Drew asked.

"You're all together," Josef clenched his jaw. "Being impure."

"No," Nikki said in disbelief. "We're just friends."

Josef narrowed his eyes at us. "You think I'm dumb?"

"Who's telling you these things?" I asked. Josef didn't break his stare, but I already knew the answer to the question. I looked at Genevieve. "What did you tell him?"

"What we've all been seeing. You're together all the time," Genevieve said.

"You're the devil," I said to her.

Genevieve gasped in mock disgust. She placed her hand over her heart and shook her head. "I told you uncle. They would deny it."

"There's nothing going on," I said.

"I won't have this," Josef said, reaching behind his back and pulling out a whip.

"No," I said, stepping back. "Please." I looked over at Mother. "Mother, please. Tell him."

She wouldn't answer me. She wouldn't even look at me.

"Mother!" I yelled for her. "Please!" She continued to sob, harder this time.

"Father," Zan said, turning his attention to his father who sat in the pew and stared at his son. He looked disgusted that Zan would choose to befriend girls like us.

"You know better, Zan," his father said.

It all happened so fast. The Guards took a step towards us, but I knew it was me he wanted to punish.

"It's me," I said to the others holding out my arms to protect them.

"October, no," Nikki said.

I turned towards her. "I'll be fine."

Nikki continued to shake her head ignoring my plea for her to stop. "No! Stop!"

The others fought them at first. I gave in, pushing the others away from me just as much as I wanted to pull them closer. The crowd remained silent as we were herded to the front of the church and made to sit on our knees. I looked up at my mother who was crying so was Brayley. He was crying so hard that his body shook. Brother Daniel stood beside their pew blocking their escape. He caught my eye and looked away.

"For as by one man's disobedience many were made sinners, so by the obedience of one shall many be made righteous…" I could hear Josef say behind me.

I held my head down and closed my eyes. I waited for the strike of the whip. I waited for the burn to fill my body. I was strong. I wouldn't let Josef get to me. I felt a hand cover mine, and I looked to see that it was Drew. We held hands. I didn't care if the others saw us. We were already guilty in their eyes.

We finally heard the screams. It wasn't recognizable at first until I looked up and saw Nikki's open mouth sucking in shaky breaths. Josef stood behind her with his hand in the air. The whip dangled from his hand, and for a moment, it looked as if he was holding a black snake. He brought the whip down on her, striking her with all his might. She screamed again and fell to the floor.

"Stop!" I yelled, getting up. I was pushed down to the floor. My cheek pressed against the cold hard floor. "Please! Stop!"

The sound of the whip whooshed through the air again, and Nikki's screams filled the air. She cried out in desperation, and I cried out to help her. I wanted Josef to take me instead.

After a while, I stopped pleading and waited for it to be over. Again and again. Josef's hand came up and down. The whip moved through the air back and forth. With each hit, Nikki's screams became more faint.

It was finally over when she stopped screaming.

CHAPTER 18

It was terrible not knowing what happened to her. I had never been apart from Nikki for more than a few days. A week went by and no word from her. No sight of her either. I had to see her. Even if I wasn't allowed to. I had come to understand that it was better to ask for forgiveness than ask for permission when it came to doing things my own way. My mother knew that Josef wouldn't be able to keep me from her for long. My mother shook her head in defeat. "One day it will be enough October," she said wearily. "One day you'll stop fighting."

I couldn't believe her. I couldn't imagine who I would be if I did.

Things had changed. After Josef's attack, if the others weren't scared of him before, they were scared now. I didn't know why, but I began to have a strange feeling. Like the calm before the storm. Something was stirring.

Since my mother was so absent, I began to get close to Sister Celine. She was nice to me, and I felt comfortable talking to her. I was helping Sister Celine with the laundry. I was pulling the linens from the line as Sister Celine hung up the clothes. My mother usually helped with the laundry, but she had been in her room all morning. No one bothered to wake her.

"Thank you for being so nice to me," I said to her one day as we hung up the laundry together.

She looked at me and smiled. Her features were delicate. "Being nice shouldn't be unusual, October. It's to be expected."

I smiled and glanced at the back door where Brother Daniel was gathering kindling. Sister Celine followed my gaze.

"You know he's happy you guys are here," she said. "The house hasn't been this alive in a long time."

"Really?" I asked. "He doesn't seem like it."

"He does," Sister Celine smiled. "He talks so much of Brayley."

"Brayley likes him too," I said. "Do you have children?"

Sister Celine shook her head. "No. I wasn't able to."

"Oh," I said suddenly, aware of how personal I had gotten. "Sorry."

"Oh, no. It's okay. We didn't really want children," Sister Celine said. "I didn't." I nodded. "What about you?"

I wrinkled my nose and shook my head. "I don't think so." Sister Celine laughed softly. I went back to pulling down the dry linens. I noticed a shape in the distance. At first it looked like a woman standing at the edge of the woods waving at me. I froze and squinted my eyes for a better look.

"Who's that?" I asked out loud. Sister Celine looked up and glanced over to the woods. She went back to hanging up clothes.

"Don't pay attention to those woods," she said sharply. "There's nothing good in them."

"I thought I saw someone."

"You didn't," Sister Celine said firmly.

I raised my eyebrow questioningly at her, but I didn't push the issue any further. I looked back at the woods but there was nothing there.

"Don't go into the woods by yourself," My father had warned me one day. "Ever."

"Why?" I had asked him. I was sitting down on the couch watching him pace the living room back and forth.

"Just don't!" my father yelled at me. It was the first time he had yelled, and it had been for a good reason.

I had gotten lost wandering inside the woods. My parents had said that it was an hour before they found me. I didn't remember what I did, but I could remember hearing their calls. I just couldn't go to them. Something had called me, and I had to answer. When I came to, I remember a long scratch on my leg. Now that I think about it, it looked more like a claw mark.

"Don't scream, Dennis," my mother said softly. "She understands."

"She doesn't," my father had said. He stopped pacing and knelt in front of me. He placed both hands on my face. I didn't understand why he was so angry or rather so scared. "Don't go into the woods by yourself. Ever."

I nodded in understanding.

Suddenly, my thoughts were interrupted by screams coming from inside of the house. I dropped what I was doing once I realized whose screams they were.

It was Brayley.

"Brayley!" I yelled, running into the house with Sister Celine on my heels. I burst through the back door into the kitchen to find his screams coming from upstairs. I raced up the stairs following the screams to my mother and Josef's bedroom. I raced inside to find Brayley standing by the side of their bed shaking her.

"Wake up!" he screamed.

"Brayley, what's wrong?" I asked, running over to him. Mother was asleep. Her body was limp as Brayley tried to shake her awake. I noticed the empty pill bottle on the nightstand.

"She won't wake up!" Brayley yelled.

"Mother?" I tapped her on the shoulder as hard as I could, but the only thing that moved was her head which tilted over to the side. White foam spilled out of her mouth and down onto her pillow. I shook her harder. "Mother!"

Suddenly, Brother Daniel rushed into the room.

"What happened?" he asked. His chest heaved up and down from his running.

"She won't wake up," I said.

Brother Daniel rushed to our side. He pressed two fingers against my mother's neck. There was a pause. "She's still alive."

I blew a sigh of relief. "How do you know?" I asked.

"She has a heartbeat," he said. "Faint, but it's there."

"What can we do?"

"You and Brayley can wait here," Brother Daniel said. He placed both hands underneath my mother, picking her up and lifting her against his chest.

"What are you going to do?" Brayley asked.

"I'm taking her to the hospital," he said. "Stay here."

"I'm not staying here," I said.

"I'll send for you two to come to the hospital just as soon as I know something," Brother Daniel said, heading towards the door.

"What about Brother Josef?" I asked.

"I don't know where he is," Brother Daniel said.

"He did this," I said.

Brother Daniel hung his head low. "I'll send for you."

"Okay. Hurry," I said, watching him leave. Brayley sat down on the bed and began to sob quietly. I sat down beside him. He rested his head against my shoulder. "She'll be okay."

"You promise?" he asked sniffing.

"I promise," I said reluctantly.

We waited for what felt like hours. I paced the room at first glancing at that empty pill bottle. I didn't want to admit it to myself, but it all made sense. The reason my mother had been shut in her room lately. She hadn't been talking to us. We barely saw her anymore. She must have sat awake a lot of nights wondering what it would be like. Wondering if she could really do it. Wondering if the pain would really end.

I stared out of the window as Brayley watched me. He bit his lip as he stared at me, but he wasn't really looking at me. He already had that dead stare that meant he had mentally checked out.

I didn't understand why she had done this. What was she to gain from taking her own life? Was it a blessing that she failed at it? Or did it just make things worse?

"Will God forgive her?"

I looked back at Brayley and shook my head. "I don't know. Do you?"

Brayley considered this. "Why would she do it? Why would she want to leave us?"

"I don't think that's the reason, Brayley," I said. "She's hurting. We all are."

"But-"

"Go to sleep, Brayley," I said, cutting him off. "Brother Daniel will send for us when he can."

Brayley obeyed, finally falling asleep in their bed. I watched him sleep, turning back to the window. I froze. It happened again. Standing in front of the edge of the woods was a figure. I blinked, and it was gone.

"Who is that?" I asked, thinking out loud.

I looked back at Brayley. I grabbed one of the lanterns by the bedside. I placed a kiss on Brayley's forehead before leaving him. On my way out of the house, I checked Josef's study, but he wasn't there. I walked over to his desk, setting the lantern down. I opened his drawers looking for anything I could use. In the right drawer, I found a knife. I grabbed it and removed the sleeve to see that it had a curved edge. I pulled up my dress and placed the knife in my boot. I opened the left drawer to find another bottle of white pills. I grabbed the pills and threw them against the wall making them spill all over the floor. I didn't care if Josef knew I had been in his study. What had happened to my mother was his fault.

I grabbed the lantern from the desk and left Josef's study. I left the door open purposefully. I wanted him to know that I had been in there.

Outside it was dark and quiet. The only sound was the crunching of snow underneath my feet. I held the lantern in front of me as I made my way to the edge of the woods. I peered into the depths of the trees, but it was too dark to see anything. I knew it was stupid going out into the woods at night alone, but I had seen someone twice. That wasn't a mistake.

"Hello?" I called out. There was silence. I stepped forward as the sound of branches snapping in the distance stopped my footsteps. "Is someone there?" I called out.

"October..." a voice whispered.

I froze at the sound of my name. "Hello?" I called out.

There was silence as I held still, looking and listening, but there was nothing.

"Who's out there?" I called out again. I waited. I lifted the lantern higher, scanning the light along the dark spaces. The light rested on a spot in the trees to my right. A dark shape lay among an empty space between the trees. I sucked in a breath and stepped forward. The dark shape darted back into the darkness. I shrieked, dropping the lantern on the ground. I hurried and picked it up. A snap of the branches indicated that something had moved, and the sound was close. Fear squeezed my throat as I struggled to scream out. Something was moving. Fast and it was getting closer.

All I could think to do was run. As fast as I could. I had to get to the house. It was like my feet weren't moving as fast as my mind. I had already imagined myself shutting the door and locking it by the time my feet hit the steps. I felt like I could breathe again as I made it onto the porch pushing the door open, entering, and locking it back.

Brayley was sitting on the bottom staircase with his wide eyes staring at me.

"What's wrong?" he asked, getting up from the stairs.

"Nothing," I said quickly, keeping my eyes on the door. "I was outside."

"Doing what?" Brayley asked.

"Stop asking me so many questions!" I snapped.

"What's wrong with you?" Brayley asked, taken aback.

"I'm sorry," I said softly. "I just got scared."

"Did you see someone out there?" he asked.

"No," I said quickly. "Everything's fine." I glanced back at the door. I half expected the doorknob to start turning, but it didn't. I couldn't tell Brayley what I had seen. I wasn't exactly sure what I had seen, but I knew I hadn't seen someone.

It was something else.

CHAPTER 19

My mother was in the hospital for over a week and hadn't woken up once. I had thought she was dead, but Brother Corbin said he could still hear a faint heartbeat. It wasn't death. He called it a coma. I didn't know what it meant. I just knew it meant that my mother wasn't waking up anytime soon.

I spent a lot of time alone at the hospital talking to her. Brayley had stopped coming after a couple of days. It was too much for him to see her like this, but I wasn't going to give up. I felt like she could hear me when I talked to her.

Despite it being his fault, Josef spent a considerable amount of time in the hospital too. Brother Daniel told me that Josef cried a lot. I knew he had a guilty conscience, but I wanted Josef to pay for what he had done. Crying about it wasn't enough. I wanted him to suffer.

One day I was at the hospital and was visited by someone I would have never expected. It was Ward.

"Hi," I said to him as he walked up to the foot of the bed. He held a vase full of purple violas. I remembered he had a garden of violas near his cabin.

"These are for her," Ward said, handing over the vase.

"Thank you," I said. I took it and placed the vase on the small table that was beside her bed. "They're pretty."

"How is she?" he asked.

I shrugged. "She's alive." I bit back tears instead focusing on one of Ward's stray curls. He had his long hair pulled back from his face. "She tried to kill herself." For some reason, saying it aloud made it more real. It hurt more, but it was the reality of it.

Ward nodded. "I heard what happened at the church. To Nikki." He shoved his hands into his pockets and rocked on his heels nervously. "How are you holding up?"

"I'm fine," I said. I glanced at my mother who was still fast asleep. Her chest moved up and down, but her body was lifeless. I would've given anything for her to wake.

"Have you seen them?" he asked.

I shook my head. Ward pursed his lips together. "I wish I had gotten the chance to tell her."

"About what?" he asked.

"About my father," I said, taking my mother's hand. "I didn't get a chance to tell my mother that I had found him. She didn't think I would, but I did. I saved him like I said I would." Ward nodded in understanding. "I don't know. Maybe it would've helped. If she had known, maybe she would've thought about it before-"

Ward stepped towards me. "Don't blame yourself. It's not your fault. It's his. He tried to leave you."

"I know," I said, pausing after realizing what Ward had said. "You're talking about my father?"

"Yes," Ward said. "If he hadn't tried to leave you, he would've never gotten caught. Brother Josef would've never gotten the chance to marry your mother and none of this-"

"Wait," I said, cutting him off. "How do you know my father tried to leave?"

Ward hesitated. "It's complicated, okay? But like I told you. I knew him."

"Who was that?" I asked my father one day.

I remembered he had the front door open and was standing by it. I stood beside him and saw that he was watching Ward walk away from our house.

"What was he doing here?" I asked him.

My father pursed his lips. "He just wanted to talk."

"About what?" I had asked.

My father had sighed. "Nothing important. He's lonely, that's all."

I watched Ward look back at us. I waved my hand, but he turned away quickly, placing his hands in his pockets and disappearing inside the woods.

I raised my eyebrow at him questioningly. "How well did you know my father?"

"Well enough," Ward said and clenched his jaw. "I have to go."

"Yeah, you should," I said bitterly. "You have a lot of nerve to come in here and tell me about my father. You wouldn't understand. It's not like he was your father."

Ward opened his mouth as if to object but then closed it. He pursed his lips, taken aback by my bitterness. He nodded at me. "Hope she gets well," he mumbled before turning to leave. I watched him walk away before turning back to my mother. I was still holding her hand. I squeezed it for reassurance.

"Mother, please wake up," I whispered to her. "Please."

I wasn't sure if I had imagined it, but I felt her squeeze back.

***

The Winter Festival marked the end of the year. The festival started that morning in church. We spent the first hours listening to a sermon from Josef. Then, we all gathered on the church grounds for the feast where the band would play, and we all danced around a fire. The best part about the festival was the food. Usually there would be tables filled with food: baskets of bread, corn pudding by the pound, fresh meat, and barrels of hot sweet cocoa. This year the festival was still on the church grounds, but our feast wasn't as hearty because of the harsh winter. We still had baskets of bread. There was no corn pudding, and our fresh meat was being used for the barrels of soup that we had to eat. We still had cocoa so I didn't mind.

Me and Brayley stood near the band drinking cocoa and watching the others as they danced around the fire which kept us warm. I shivered a little from the cold. I scanned the crowd for Nikki. I still hadn't seen her, and I was getting worried.

"Maybe you should go see her," Brayley said.

I shook my head. "No. I don't want to cause any more trouble."

"What are you going to do?" asked Brayley. "I don't like it here anymore. Everything's changing."

I turned to him and placed a hand on his shoulder. "Hey, everything will be fine."

Brayley frowned. "No, it won't."

"Is everything okay?" a voice asked, walking up to us.

I saw that it was Sister Celine. She had a worried look on her face as she looked us over particularly Brayley who had begun to sulk. I shook my head.

"Come," she said to him, holding her hand out for him to take. Brayley took it without hesitation. "You want to go home?" Brayley nodded. She glanced at me, and I nodded in agreement.

"How is he feeling?" Brother Daniel asked, walking up to me once Brayley and Sister Celine's figures disappeared among the crowd.

"He'll be alright," I said. "He just needs to accept it."

"She's his mother," Brother Daniel said. "It's understandable."

"She tried to kill herself. It's clear she doesn't want to be with us," I said. "Without my father. She really couldn't see how we all fit together."

"Don't say that," Brother Daniel said. "You don't know that."

"It's true," I said. "I'm tired of people making excuses for why they did what they did or who they are. Like you."

Brother Daniel raised an eyebrow at me. "Me? What does that mean?"

"Who are you?" I asked, turning to him. "Just tell me. I can handle the truth."

Brother Daniel snorted. "Can you? You're tough. Don't get me wrong. We all know that about you. But there are things about this place that would scare even you."

I thought back to that thing I saw in the woods. "Like what?"

Brother Daniel opened his mouth to answer but then decided against it.

I looked away from him to the band where I caught the attention of Drew. He smiled at me, and I smiled back. I hadn't been able to be with him, and I wanted nothing more but to dance with him. It would make me feel better. He was like a light in all of this darkness.

"You're right," Brother Daniel suddenly said. "I'm not who I say I am."

I looked back at him. "Then who are you?"

"Well…" Brother Daniel hesitated again. "I'm-"

Suddenly, he was interrupted by a scream.

CHAPTER 20

Following the scream, the crowd turned their attention near the cemetery to see Sister Martha, one of the older women of the community, standing with her arms held out. Her body was engulfed in flames. Her stance made her look like a burning angel. The crowd screamed as everyone got out of her path. I gasped.

"October!" she called out to me. She stepped in my direction, leaving behind trails of burning grass. A wide smile spread across her face. "Harvest is upon you."

"Oh God," I whispered. I covered my mouth to keep from screaming.

"Harvest is upon you!" Sister Martha yelled in the air.

"Get her out of here!" I could hear Josef yell over the panicked crowd.

Brother Daniel grabbed my arm, pulling me away from Sister Martha. Terrified screams filled the air, but I couldn't close my eyes. I had to see. The pain must have finally gotten to her because Sister Martha groaned and dropped to her knees. She began to crawl, reaching her black burnt hand towards me. I could smell her burning skin even though I was several feet away from her.

"Harvest-" her cries were cut short by the sound of a gunshot silencing the crowd. Her lifeless body dropped to the ground. The flames continued to dance off of her dead corpse.

"Get her out of here!" Josef yelled again to Brother Daniel. The crowd was in shock as they stared at the burning body. Everyone was visibly shaken. My knees buckled, and Brother Daniel caught me from falling.

"No! Wait!" I yelled.

"We have to go!" Brother Daniel said.

"Wait!" I yelled, but I was no match for Brother Daniel who placed his arm around my waist and pulled me from the church grounds. I fought against him at first but finally stopped. I was led to the barn where Brother Daniel shut the door and locked it, pulling the wooden bar against the door handle.

"What the hell was that?" I yelled at him.

"October-"

"What's going on?" my father's voice interrupted him. I shrieked and looked up to see him standing over the railing. "What happened?"

"Why don't you ask him?" I said angrily.

"Danny, what's going on?" my father asked, turning his attention to Brother Daniel.

"Nothing-"

"Nothing?" I asked, cutting him off. "A woman just lit herself on fire in front of everyone! What was that about?"

Brother Daniel held his hand out. "Just calm down."

"Calm down?" I asked. "You want me to calm down?"

"What happened?" my father asked.

I turned to see my father coming down the ladder. He jumped down onto the ground and walked over to us.

"You should be hiding," Brother Daniel said to him.

"My daughter needs me," my father said, walking up to me. He placed both hands on my arms, steadying me. "Tell me what happened."

"We were at the Winter Festival. Sister Martha lit herself on fire. She called out to me," I said, rambling. "She said 'Harvest is upon you.' She meant me. Harvest is upon me. What does that mean?"

My father exchanged glances with Brother Daniel. "I don't know."

"No more secrets," I said firmly.

My father avoided my gaze. He shook his head. "I don't know."

"Oh God," I pulled away from him. "Something isn't right. First the woman. Now this. Something is wrong."

My father raised an eyebrow at me. "What woman?"

"The woman in the woods. I keep seeing her."

My father glanced at Brother Daniel again.

"Why do you keep looking at him?" I asked him. "You know something."

"October-"

"Don't keep lying to me!" I yelled at him. "What's going on?"

My father and Brother Daniel exchanged glances once again and suddenly I figured it out. Their eyes.

"Wait," I said, backing up from both of them. "You two…"

"…are brothers," my father finished for me. I was speechless. My father held out his hand to keep me calm. "I know. It sounds crazy, but Danny is my brother."

"Older brother," Brother Daniel chimed in.

"Why didn't you say anything?" I asked Brother Daniel. Brother Daniel opened his mouth to speak but was interrupted.

"Danny betrayed me. That's why he didn't tell you," my father said.

Brother Daniel scoffed. "No, I didn't."

"You did," my father said, turning on him. "We were going to get away from here. Me and you, but you turned your back on me. You joined him!"

"There's nothing out there for us!" Brother Daniel said, raising his voice. "This is what we know. This is what we're good at."

My father shook his head. "That's not true. You didn't even try. You've always done everything he's asked of you without question including-" Something made my father stop. He glanced at me.

"What? Including what?" I asked.

"Dennis-" Brother Daniel said, stepping towards my father.

"No," my father said, stopping him. "She deserves to know."

"Know what?" I asked.

Brother Daniel shook his head and turned away from us. He pinched the bridge of his nose in frustration just like my father.

"Know what?" I repeated myself.

"He's the one who…" my father was hesitant but then sighed. "Danny is the one who took you."

"What?"

I didn't remember much from that time, but what I remember were his eyes. Now that I remembered it, they were the same kind of eyes like my father. He had those kinds of eyes that crinkled around the edges. They were nice eyes. The kind of eyes that were filled with something. A promise. A dream. Maybe that's why I went with him. I didn't know then but he had taken me away from everything and led me somewhere where I was nothing.

"Is that true?" I asked him.

Brother Daniel didn't turn to face me. "Yes."

"Why?"

"I was following orders."

"Why would you bring me here?"

"Yeah Danny. Why would you bring her here?" my father repeated after me, but it was more like a taunt instead of a question.

"Don't," Brother Daniel said.

The lock on the wooden door began to rattle as someone pounded on the door.

"Hide," Brother Daniel said to my father.

My father nodded and looked around the room. A pile of hay was in the corner of the barn. My father rushed over to hide behind it. The wooden door continued to rattle.

"Who do you think it is?" I asked Brother Daniel.

He shook his head and walked towards the door unlocking it. I held my breath as he opened the door to reveal Drew, Nikki, Zan, and Ward standing on the other side. I heaved a sigh of relief. My father came out from hiding behind the hay.

"Nikki?" I called out to her. She gave me a small smile. We embraced. Nikki held me for a while as we cried. "I'm so sorry. I didn't mean for that to happen to you. It should've been me."

"Don't say that," Nikki said, pulling herself away from me. She brushed her thumb against my cheek, wiping away my tears. "It's not your fault. I'm okay. Really. It hurts, but I'm okay."

I nodded. I looked at Drew, and he took me in his arms. It felt good to rest against his chest.

"You okay?" Drew asked, whispering in my ear. He stroked my hair.

"I'm fine," I said. Drew pulled back from me and studied me.

"Ward?" my father said, staring at Ward.

We all stared at them. Ward stared at my father. My father stared at Ward. Something passed between the two of them. Now looking at the both of them, I was starting to wonder just how deep their connection was.

"Nice to see you, Brother Dennis," Ward mumbled.

My father opened his mouth to say something else but then hesitated. He glanced at me. Zan cleared his throat to break the awkward silence.

"I bet no one saw that coming," Zan said, rubbing his hand through his hair. "That was-"

"Scary," Nikki finished for him. Zan nodded.

"It just doesn't make sense," Drew said. "Why would she set herself on fire?"

"None of this makes sense," Ward said.

"Well there is one thing we know for sure," Zan said.

"What?" I asked him.

"All of this is about you," Zan said. "All of it. Don't you want to know why?"

"No," my father said firmly. "October needs to worry about getting out of here. That's it."

"He's right," I said to Zan. "I just want to get out. I want all of us to get out."

"Look," Brother Daniel said, holding his hand to silence us. "Can we just stop and think for a second? Where would you go? No one on the outside knows about us."

"Somewhere," I said. "Anywhere is better than here."

"This is all of our homes," Brother Daniel said. "Whether you like it or not."

I turned on him. "We're getting out of here whether you like it or not, and I need your help. You owe me."

Brother Daniel opened his mouth to object but stopped. He looked away because he knew I was right.

CHAPTER 21

It surprised me that everyone went on with their lives as if the incident at the Winter Festival had been normal, but I couldn't. I searched the church grounds looking for any signs of burned leaves or burned grass. I searched the headstones for Sister Martha's grave. Any sign that I hadn't imagined what had happened. I tried to keep talking about it with my father, but he offered no assistance.

"Why do you want to keep talking about it?" my father asked me.

"Because I want to understand."

"I know, but it's not important," my father said. "It's not going to help us escape."

I decided that if my father would be no help, then I would have to look to someone else. I went to Drew. He had been there. I remembered his terrified expression as he watched from the stage. Maybe he could help me figure out what it all meant.

When I walked into the Plaza, I saw that all the shops were still closed. I walked up to the Keegan's shop and knocked on it. There was no answer. Drew hadn't been at home which was why I had come here. Where else could he have been? I stared at the door and waited a few more seconds, but no one answered the door. I walked over to the shop's window and peered inside with my hands cupped against the cold glass window.

Drew was inside standing behind the counter, and he wasn't alone. Standing in front of the counter was Genevieve. He spoke to her and smiled. Genevieve nodded her head then placed her hand on the counter. Drew placed his hand on top of hers. I gasped. For some reason, I must have thought I was invisible because when they looked over to the window at me, it didn't register that they could see me. Drew's mouth dropped. Even Genevieve looked guilty.

I turned away from the window and ran as fast as I could. I could feel the tears form in my eyes, and I couldn't let them see me cry.

When I went back into the house, I was ready to be caught with tears running down my face by Brayley or Brother Daniel or worse Josef. But no one was around. I sat on the bottom of the stairs and cried until his voice forced me to wipe the remaining tears from my face.

"October?"

Josef walked around the side of the staircase and stared at me blankly.

"Brother Josef," I said, standing up.

"How are you?" he asked.

"I'm fine," I said.

"Have you seen your mother lately?" Josef asked.

"Yes," I said.

"Do you think she's going to wake up any time soon?"

I shrugged. "I don't know, Brother Josef. Will she? I mean you're the expert on all of this. What does God say?"

Josef clenched his jaw. "Don't. I was only trying to-"

"Trying to do what?" I asked, interrupting him. "You've done enough."

"Excuse me?" Josef said, taking a small step towards me.

"My mother tried to kill herself because of you." Josef opened his mouth to speak, but I cut him off again. "You didn't need to hurt her to get to me."

Josef took another menacing step towards me. "What did you say to me?"

"You heard me," I snarled.

Josef scoffed. "You think you have it all figured out, don't you? If you knew anything, you would know that the last person I would hurt would be your mother. I didn't mean for this to happen."

"You gave her the pills!"

"She wanted them!" Josef pinched the bridge of his nose and closed his eyes. "After the first time, she kept asking, and she wouldn't stop. I warned her that she was taking too many but-"

"If she dies, it's because of you."

The shock came after the sting. I placed my hand on my burning cheek and laughed. I bet he had been wanting to do that forever. Josef looked down at his hand in disbelief as if he hadn't realized what he had done.

"You didn't give me a choice," Josef said.

I snorted as he walked off.

"Brother Josef?" I called out to him.

He stopped in his tracks, not turning around.

"He made us happy."

Even with his back turned, I could see that I had struck a nerve. Josef walked into the living room, leaving me alone.

I sat back down on the stairs, thinking about Josef's hit.

"How does it feel?" my father had asked me.

I remembered I had been twelve and it was the first time that I had been hit. I talked back to Sister Jennifer in the classroom, and she had went across my face so quickly that I couldn't do anything but cry. The entire class had witnessed it, and from that day on, I had vowed to never let them see me cry again.

"I'm fine," I said to my father. He put a finger under my chin and lifted my head up to take a closer look.

"Don't let them scare you," my father said. "Ever. No matter what they do."

I nodded. "Yes, Father."

"What happened?" a voice shocked me from my daze.

I looked behind me to see Brayley standing at the top of the stairs. "What do you want?"

"I heard what happened at the Winter Festival," Brayley said. "Are you okay?"

"I'm fine," I said.

"No, you're not," Brayley said. "Sister Martha lit herself on fire. In front of everyone. For you. Why would she do that?"

"I don't know," I said. "But I have to tell you something. It's about Brother Daniel."

"What about him?" Brayley asked, coming down the stairs. He sat beside me.

"I don't think you should trust him," I said.

"Why not?"

"He's the one who brought us here. To this place," I said. "We're here because of him."

Brayley considered this for a moment. "Well, he's been nice to us...and he's family."

"How do you know that?" I asked him.

"He told me," Brayley said. I raised an eyebrow at him. "Didn't think I could keep a secret, huh? Especially from you."

I opened my mouth to object, but he stopped me.

"I can handle the truth, October," Brayley said.

"I didn't say you couldn't."

We were interrupted by the sound of knocking on the door.

"I got it," I said, getting up from the stairs. I walked to the front door and opened it. Drew was standing on the other side. He had his hands in his pockets, and he looked up at me with sorry eyes.

"Hey," he said.

"You can't be here."

"I owe you an explanation," Drew said.

I stepped outside onto the porch, closing the door. I crossed my arms against my chest. "For what?"

"For what you saw. With me and Genevieve. It wasn't like that," he said.

"Then what was it?"

"She needed someone to talk to. She's going through stuff," Drew said. "That's all it was. I promise."

I sighed. "I don't feel sorry for her, but I understand. She trusts you. I trust you."

Drew stepped towards me. I watched as he leaned down and kissed me on my forehead softly. I closed my eyes and could feel his hand slip into mine.

"I'm sorry," he whispered.

I opened my eyes and looked up at him. He leaned down again, and I reached up to kiss him. I wrapped my arms around his neck, pulling him closer to me. I dug my hands into his hair. He pulled me tighter.

"October!" a voice yelled across the lawn. We broke apart and looked across the lawn to see Nikki and Zan running over to us.

"What's wrong?" I asked, stepping down from the porch.

"Something's going on at the fence!" Nikki said out of breath from running.

The front door opened, and I looked back to see Josef step out.

"What's going on?" Josef asked.

I could see that Nikki took a step back.

"There's something going on at the fence," Zan said, stepping in front of her.

I raised an eyebrow at Drew, and he shrugged his shoulders. We followed Nikki and Zan to the front of the fence with Josef following behind us.

The entire community had gathered at the front gates as if waiting to be ushered into heaven. Saints and Sinners alike stared wide eyed towards something that captivated their attention.

"What's going on?" Zan asked one of the sisters.

"Someone saw a person on the other side of the fence, and they started talking with them. She said she was looking for someone," the sister said.

"Who?" Drew asked.

She glanced at me and shook her head. "I don't know."

We pushed through the crowd, and when we got to the front, we could see what all the fuss was about.

A woman stood outside of the gates. Josef rushed over to the gates, hiding my view of her.

"Everyone get back!" Josef yelled over the panic of the crowd. I could hear the whispers, and most people were confused.

"They found us."

"I thought we were protected."

"What does she want?"

For the first time, Josef had lost control, and it showed. His cheeks were red from embarrassment. His eyes darted over us, and he looked disheveled. No one was listening to him. This was his worst nightmare.

"Get back I said!" Josef yelled once more. He pulled a gun from behind his back, held it straight into the air, and fired. I sucked in a loud breath. The crowd drew back, and I closed my eyes as the shout rang loudly in my ear. It was finally silent.

"Who is that?" Nikki whispered.

I shook my head. Josef tucked the gun behind him and held his hand out to silence us.

"Will everyone please calm down?" Josef yelled.

"Who is that?" I could hear a voice ask from the crowd. It sounded like Brother Jack.

Josef took a step forward, and I was finally able to see. My jaw dropped.

"Oh my God," I whispered once I saw the figure on the other side of the fence. She was here.

"She has your eyes," Drew whispered to me.

SPRING

CHAPTER 22

The snow began to fade on the ground. The pond returned like it always did, and the cornfields returned to normal. We even saw the return of brightly colored flowers. Their cracked brown roots turned to ordinary green. Everything felt like it always did except for the punishment. If the stranger's appearance was a revelation, then everything else that followed was leading up to the apocalypse.

Around the community I was stared at. Everyone knew who she was and who she had come for. Brother Daniel warned me that everyone was keeping a close watch on me. Even more closely than they already did. Josef had made an announcement that we were not to go near the fence or face punishment. If anyone was caught talking to the stranger, they would be deemed heretics, and heretics were burned at the stake.

Even though I hadn't been to see her, I dreamt about her. I dreamed about coming face to face with her. My dreams revealed that her face was no different from mine. I wanted to speak to her. I wanted to know if she was really who I believed her to be.

With the harsh winter over, we returned to school. Sister Jennifer was back to her old antics, picking me to blame for everything and believing every word her daughter said about me. We also returned to working in the cornfields. Everyone, including Saints, were put to work filling buckets of corn. We had to make up for lost time, and there weren't enough Sinners to do it. Everyone knew the corn was our lifeline, so some of the Saints didn't mind. The more corn we picked, the more supplies we were able to get. The hunger had stopped for most of us, and no one, not even the Saints, wanted to feel what that was like again.

"You okay?" Nikki asked Zan who had sworn underneath his breath. He and Drew had joined us during the weeks that we were all expected to help. It was nice having someone else carry the buckets for once.

Zan sucked his finger and shook his head. "Is this what you used to do everyday?"

Nikki smiled and nodded. Drew chuckled.

"It's not that bad," Drew said. "It feels good getting your hands dirty."

"Yeah, no," Zan said, wiping his hands on his pants. He picked up the bucket spilling some of the kernels on the ground.

"Careful," Nikki said to him.

Zan sighed and began picking up the spilled kernels. "Does it even matter if we pick this? We're going to be gone soon anyway."

"Shh!" I said, glancing around. "Not if they hear you."

"Is everything okay?" a voice asked in the distance. We looked down the row to see Brother Jack watching us. My stomach dropped once I realized that we had been caught together. I could hear Drew curse underneath his breath. Nikki drew in a breath. Brother Jack tilted his head to the side. "Always you four, huh?"

I opened my mouth to object to say anything to get us in the clear. This time it would be me to take the fall.

"Just get back to work," Brother Jack mumbled and disappeared among the rows. I heaved a sigh of relief. I looked back to see Zan removing his hand from Nikki's back. He was protecting her as well. There was silence as the unspoken guilt between us returned.

Zan finally spoke up. "I'm just saying. You need to find a way to talk to her. She's here for you after all."

"I'm working on it," I said to him.

"You know now that their stomachs are full, they're eating out of the palms of his hand again," Zan said.

"Zan, I know."

"Do you? Because Annual Harvest is coming and that's not a good thing for any of us," Zan continued. "You heard Sister Martha-"

"Stop," Drew said, cutting him off. Zan narrowed his eyes at him but didn't continue.

"Zan, she knows," Nikki said, placing a hand on his arm. Zan shrugged her off.

"Don't trust the Elders," my father had said one day during Cleansing. "Not even their children."

I remember watching Josef as he called the Elders one by one to the tub. It seemed like they were enjoying themselves. I watched as Brother Alex smiled and laughed as Josef dunked him into the pool of water. The rest of us looked at them with grim expressions. This was not fun and games to us.

"Why not?" I had asked him.

"They're just as much in control as he is. Without them, he wouldn't know what to do. Some of them have been around since the beginning," my father had warned me. "Blue Corn would be nothing without them."

"You know, Zan," I said, turning to face him. "I never understood why you're with us. Drew, I get. But you Zan, no. Why does a kid like you want to get out so badly? You're an Elder's child? You have everything."

Zan's cheeks flushed. "My life isn't perfect, okay?"

I looked over at Nikki to see that she was chewing on her lip nervously as she looked back and forth between the two of us. "How?"

"It's complicated, okay?" Zan said. "But I remember. My father. His wrists. I remember seeing the marks. I never asked what they were, but I just had a feeling that something was wrong."

I pursed my lips together unsure how I felt about Zan. Something bad must've happened to him for him to turn on his father. He was an Elder's child. He was guaranteed a perfect life here but even I could see that he wanted to get out.

"I love my parents, but I don't want to be a part of this anymore," he said to me. "It isn't right, and I see that now." I nodded. "Plus, I don't believe in any of it," Zan further explained at the sight of my furrowed eyebrows, "I don't believe in a god, his god, God at all."

I raised an eyebrow and glanced at Drew. He shrugged.

"Don't worry about it," Zan said, picking up the spilled kernels. "I want out and I'm going to make sure we get away from this place."

We all exchanged glances. Nikki pursed her lips and shook her head for me not to probe any further. I looked back at Zan. His attention was back on picking the corn, but his cheeks were still red.

After we were done, we went our separate ways. Drew went in the direction of the Plaza. Nikki and Zan went in another. I went back home. I was in my room when Brayley found me. He hadn't really talked to me about the stranger, but the look on his face meant that was about to change, especially after I had told him about finding our father.

Something memorable happened when I thought back to the reunion of Brayley and our father. Brayley had collided into my father with a sense of wonder yet relief. I looked upon them content with my decision to finally tell him about our father but a little sad at how we had come to be like this. When was the exact moment that our family had been broken? Either it was when my father had left us waiting for him or when my mother decided to follow the leader and uproot us from everything we had been taught. Or was it always broken? Was our happiness together only an illusion? At that moment, I didn't care. Whatever had made us happy, I had wanted it back.

"Can I sit?" he asked.

I turned to see him standing in the doorway. "Yeah," I said, bending down to unlace my boots. Brayley sat beside me. He had that worried look on his face. "What's wrong?"

"They've been talking about her," Brayley said. "I overheard Garrett say he thinks she's bringing more outsiders to kill us."

I raised an eyebrow at such an absurd assumption. "We don't know why she's here," I said. "But she's not here to hurt us."

"You think so?" Brayley asked.

"I know so," I said.

"She's pretty," Brayley said with a small smile. "She looks like us," I nodded. "Is she our mother?"

I nodded slowly. "Yes."

Brayley considered this. He seemed to light up at this revelation.

I reached over and opened the top drawer on my nightstand. I dug out the photo I took from my mother before we lived with Josef. It was the photo of my real mother and us. "Look," I said, handing it to Brayley. "I found this in our old house." He took it and studied it.

"I would go with her," Brayley said to me, staring at the photo. I was taken aback. I was afraid Brayley was too attached to this place. Him and our mother had become so close. I didn't know if he would leave her if it came down to it.

"You would?" I asked him. "What about Mother?"

Brayley considered this and looked at me. "October, I love Mother. A lot. But it's you I would follow." I stared at him. He was growing up, and I hadn't even realized just how much. "What will Brother Josef do to her?" he asked, staring back at the photo.

"Nothing," I said to him. "He's bound to this place just like the rest of us. He can't get to her."

"I hope that's true," Brayley mumbled.

"I want to go talk to her. I want to ask her why she's here," I said.

"It's simple," Brayley said, smiling. "She's come to save us."

CHAPTER 23

"It's sad, really," Sister Velma, one of the nurses, said to me. She cocked her head to the side looking at me with pity. "Sometimes the world is full of sorrow. But, October, your mother will be fine. It is the Lord's will."

"She's dying, isn't she?" I asked. "Brother Corbin won't say." I was sitting beside the bed, holding my mother's hand. It was terrible. My mother was shrinking underneath the gown that she was wearing, and whatever life that had been there before was gone. She looked like a shell of herself. I was trying not to seem distraught, but I had chewed my bottom lip so much that I could taste the metallic taste of blood on my tongue.

Sister Velma pursed her lips but didn't answer the question. That told me everything I needed to know. "I lost my little girl ten years ago. She was a baby. She had gotten really sick," she said. "Her face is starting to fade. But I know she's still here with me."

"How do you know?"

Sister Velma shrugged. "Just a feeling. Like when the wind blows or when I catch a scent of something. I know it's her. Your mother will still be there October. Just in a different way. It's best to accept that now."

I didn't understand it, but the nurse had made death seem so fantastical. I furrowed my eyebrows together, confused and watched as she walked away from me to take care of an elderly man who was coughing and vomiting at one of the other beds.

I was glad that Brayley had been spared today from seeing our mother like this. I knew she wouldn't have wanted him here. He was so accustomed to her beauty and her flushed cheeks that the image of her dried skin and grayish hue would've given him nightmares. It was best he hadn't decided to come with me today.

I took a deep breath and laid my head on her chest. Her heartbeat was faint. Soft like the tiny patter of rain on a tin roof. My mother was giving up. I could feel it. Even though her heart was still beating, she was barely hanging on. No matter what I thought I knew, this life was too unbearable for her.

One of the sisters at the church had asked me if I was lonely because of my mother or if I was feeling scared without her. I had told them yes, I was lonely and yes, I was scared.

"You're a brave girl," the sister had replied.

It was the nicest compliment any one of them had ever said to me.

The Elders' wives came to visit us. I didn't know why, but it felt like they knew that this was some sort of finality. They had clear intentions to make sure that their presence would be a sign of support yet they had timid smiles and uneasy hands as they trembled to wrap their arms around me. I took their support humbly, showing no signs of dissatisfaction, but I had the slightest notion that it was all for show. They buttered the bread with hatefulness, and their hugs soothed me in disgrace. If good works were the key to a charitable acceptance, then these women had secured their future. But I was doubtful and since they only came to visit my mother just that one time, their motives were all but godly.

"They're all corneaters," I remembered my father muttering to me one day after church. We had witnessed the remarkable during a service of revival. One of the Elder's wives had announced her pregnancy after twenty years of trying with Brother Ray. They were a couple in their fifties and as devout to Brother Josef as he was to them.

"What's a corneater?" I had asked him.

"They don't even care what they're being fed," my father said, sneering at them. "Madness. Delusion. As long as they have a place at the table, they'll keep eating even if they know it's not real."

I stepped into a big pile of melting snow. I passed the schoolhouse to see that Ward was shoveling snow away from the steps where it had gathered. He looked up at me and gave me a tight lipped smile. I thought about asking him to come with me to see the stranger, but I stopped myself. The last time me and Ward talked it hadn't gone well. He was so hard to read sometimes, and I couldn't understand him. But I knew I wanted to.

I disappeared into the cornstalks. It seemed like they were coming alive a little bit more everyday. Today their stalks were dyed halfway brown. I brushed against their leaves. They were hard and rough.

I crouched down once I neared the edge of the stalks. My heart pounded. I pushed a leaf back so that I could see the clearing. It was strangely empty. There were no farmers or Guards around.

I took a deep breath and ran to the fence. I didn't look back, not once. I rushed to the front of the fence and grabbed the bars steadying my breath as I looked out at the open world. There were just trees, but it was something. There was a world out there, and I wanted to see all of it.

"You're here," the stranger appeared from the trees. We stared at each other for a second. The sight of her was a revelation. It was like looking into my future. Her skin was dark and satiny like mine, and she had the same chocolate colored eyes. Her hair was big and curly like mine.

"It's you," She reached her hand through the small slits in the fence. I took it and held on tightly to it. It was the first time I'd felt my mother's touch since I was a child. "How did you find me?"

"It's a long story," she said. "But this place is popular where I'm from. Strange, but popular. Where's your brother?"

"He's here," I said. "With me."

"How is he?" she asked.

"He's fine," I said and smiled because I couldn't hold it in anymore. "I can't believe you're here. I thought you would never find us."

"I never stopped looking for you," she said.

I stepped closer. She moved closer as well, pressing her forehead against the metal bars. I pressed my forehead against hers and closed my eyes. "I'm so glad you're here."

"What is it like in there?" she asked. "Are they hurting you?"

"It's hard," I said. "For the both of us."

I could hear her suck in a breath.

"I'm going to get you out," she said.

"Good," I said. "I want to leave. We want to leave."

She nodded. "Good."

I pulled my head back and looked at her. "I can't explain everything to you right now. But I'll do anything to get out of here. This place is bad,"

"I agree," my mother said. "But you have to trust me."

I nodded. "I do. I have so many questions."

"And I have your answers," she said. "What do they call you here?"

I hesitated. What was my name? I never considered that October wasn't really my name. It was all I knew, and it never crossed my mind that there had been something different.

"October."

"October?" she said and chuckled. "That's cute. And your brother?"

"Brayley."

She took it in and smiled. "I like that."

"What are our real names?" I asked.

My mother gave me a small smile. "I'll tell you one day. But I think October suits you."

"What's your name?" I asked her.

"Renee," she said. "Renee Anderson."

Anderson. My real last name was Anderson. I liked the sound of it.

I looked behind me at the sound of the corn stalks rustling. I didn't spot anyone, so I figured it was just the wind. I couldn't afford to get caught. "I can't stay long. I'm afraid they'll catch me."

"I know," she said. "But come back. I'll be here every night waiting for you." I nodded. She squeezed my hand one more time before backing away from the fence. "Give your brother a kiss for me."

"Renee?" I called out to her to hear what it felt like. I wasn't yet at the stage to call her mother, but I guess she didn't mind because she stopped and smiled at me. "Please don't leave us."

She shook her head. "I'll never leave you. Ever. This isn't going to be easy, but I promise I'm going to get you out."

CHAPTER 24

I turned from the fence and headed back into the cornfields. The sun hung low in the sky, and I knew that nightfall would be soon. I had to hurry if I wanted to get back home before dark. I hated being in the cornfields by myself, especially at night.

I thought back to my conversation with Renee. This stranger was my mother, and she was everything that I had imagined her to be. I had always thought that she had left us to be here, that she hadn't wanted to be bothered with us anymore. I had already accepted that we would never see her again. Now she was here in the flesh. Brayley might have been right. She was here to save us.

Daylight turned quickly into twilight, and my steady walk turned into a brisk walk. A silent panic was starting to set in. I paused to catch my breath and wondered if anyone had figured out that I had left worship. Brayley had promised to cover for me, but if Josef were to have Brayley questioned, I knew he wouldn't be able to stand up to him for long.

I knew I wasn't far from the house, but the cornfields seemed to stretch on for miles. An endless sea of green. I turned to look behind me as the glimpse of a figure moving between the rows caught me off guard. I gasped and froze. When I was finally able to move, I began to back up slowly.

My mind is playing tricks on me, I thought. *It's been a long day and I'm tired. I just have to keep moving and I will be home soon unless...*

The sound of rustling in the fields made me snap my head to the right where the noise was coming from. There was nothing there, but I could feel like there was something around me. I took one more step back and turned to run but was stopped in my tracks.

I ran into the scarecrow that looked over the fields. Black birds scattered away from it and flew up into the sky in a flurry of wings and caws. I stared up at the scarecrow at its wide almost devilish grin cut out against its straw stuffed face. I swallowed and waited for another noise to startle me, but it didn't.

I realized that it was almost dark. I ran past the scarecrow burying myself further into the cornfields. Suddenly, I could feel it. A presence. Without even looking, I could feel something reaching out for me. Something was coming after me, and I didn't want to look back to see it. My breath quickened.

"*October...*"

Something rustled behind me. That's when I turned around and finally saw it. It had finally been revealed to me.

It was a woman. She was behind me moving at a crooked pace as her knees bent to move her forward. Her gray hair was matted and hung down in wispy strands. Her skin was gray, and it was wrinkled and dried. She was naked, but her crooked pace shocked me more than her nakedness. Her limbs were at crooked angles. Her wrinkled skin barely covered her bones. Her sagging breasts couldn't even hide the jutting of her ribs.

My eyes grew wide, and I screamed. At that moment, I didn't care that I had skipped worship or that someone would think that I had been at the fence. I just wanted someone to hear me and find me before whatever this was had its way with me. I turned back, taking a stumbling step to the ground. I cried out. I pressed my hand against the ground trying to pull myself up, but it was slippery. The dirt was thick and slightly muddy, so I couldn't get a good grip to pull myself up.

A burning pain cut into my ankle, and I was yanked by my foot. I looked back to see that the woman's long bony fingers had gripped my ankle. Her flesh was cold. I tried to kick free, but her grip tightened and cut more into my skin. The pressure of her grip felt like my ankle would pop at any second. I thrashed and wiggled covering myself with mud and dirt. The woman's long fingers continued its way up my legs pulling up my dress. I got one look at her face, and I screamed again.

The woman was crouched over me now. Her eyes were bloodshot and sunken in which made her skeletal face more terrifying. I closed my eyes, and I could feel her bony fingers touch my cheek. I flinched at her caress.

I could feel cold dry lips rub against my ear as her raspy voice whispered, *"Harvest is upon you."*

I yelled out for help. The woman's grip loosened. I opened my eyes as she lifted her head. I waited for her to finish me, but her eyes were staring at something ahead of us. I used the distraction to press my hands against her face, my fingers poking into her eyes. The woman yelped and backed away as she crawled away from me. I kicked her in the face and scrambled up running into a hooded figure who grabbed me by the arms.

"Now that we've got your attention," the voice snarled, throwing me back onto the ground.

I yelled out as a sharp pain went through my back. The figure jumped down on me straddling me to the ground.

"Get off!" I yelled. There was a flash of silver as the hooded figure pulled a knife from behind him and held it to my throat. I yelped but stopped moving. "Please!" The hooded figure pressed the knife harder against my throat. I could feel the knife digging into my skin. With his other hand, the figure yanked my dress up revealing my underwear. I tried to move, but his weight on me didn't help. "Please don't. Please!"

He began to unbutton his pants. I looked away. I could imagine where this was headed, and I couldn't let him do it. I turned my head away, cutting my neck in the process and pushed him off of me with all my might. He fell back on the ground. I hurried up off the ground, placing my hand on my neck. I could feel the warm liquid, but the blood didn't scare me and I didn't feel anything. I ran. I was almost out of the cornfields. Someone was bound to have heard something or seen me running.

I screamed as I ran into someone else. I fought against them.

"October, it's me!" Ward's voice said. He held the lantern up to his face, and when I realized it was him, I relaxed, finally catching my breath. "Oh my God. You're bleeding."

I began to cry hysterically. "They were after me. First the woman and then a man-"

"There's no one there."

"What?" I spun around to see the row was empty. "They were there. Someone attacked me."

"Come here," Ward took me into his arms. We stood there for a moment as I caught my breath sobbing into his shirt.

"I'm scared, Ward," I said shakily. I balled my hands into his shirt. I could feel how wet it was getting from my tears, but I couldn't help it.

"You're safe now," I could feel his hand on the back of my head rubbing my hair. "You're safe with me," he whispered in my ear.

CHAPTER 25

Waking up in the middle of the night, I felt like I was relieving the attack all over again. I yelled for Ward, and he appeared to me to bring me comfort whether in the form of extra blankets, a warm cup of tea, or himself. He wrapped his arms around me, and I buried my face in his chest. There were no words between us, but it was enough. We had fallen asleep together sometime in the night. I didn't remember how I ended up in his bed, but later that night, I could feel his warm hands resting on the curve of my hip.

It was the best sleep I had gotten in a long time. The sun seemed to shine more brightly casting an orange dreamlike glow over the room. The side Ward had been sleeping on was empty.

I got out of bed and walked down the hall, stopping at the doorway. The inside of his cabin was small but neat. The walls were made of wood panels, and there was a small table in the middle of the living room. Beside the fireplace was a crate filled with kindling. In the kitchen, there was a window above the kitchen sink that looked over the woods.

Ward was in the kitchen leaning over the counter drinking from a small cup. "Goodmorning."

"Goodmorning."

"Do you want to talk about it?" he asked.

"No."

And that was all he ever mentioned about it. It was our secret nonetheless but reassuring that what I had been feeling wasn't mine alone. He had been feeling it too. It was a different feeling than when I was with Drew. Drew's affections were direct. A touch of the hand meant that I was on his mind. A kiss meant that he wanted my body. His looks told me that there was no one else. With Ward, there were no touches here or there. Just a subtle glance but it meant everything. When his hard voice spoke to me, his affection hit me harder in a way that Drew's tenderness would never. It was powerful, but so soft at the same time.

"You said there was a woman?" Ward asked.

"She wasn't human," I said to him. "Or used to be. I don't know."

Ward furrowed his brow together confused. "And there was a man?"

"He was real," I said. "I could feel him. He was as human as I was, but she was something else. Who is she?"

Ward shrugged. "I don't know."

I felt like I could cry again, and I did. Ward wrapped me in a hug, and I buried my face into his chest. "She wasn't human."

He rubbed my back, and the memory of the attack flooded my mind once again.

When I felt like I had overstayed my welcome, I left him.

I left with regret. Regret that I wanted to stay longer and regret that I couldn't stay longer. But if I didn't get back, the word would surely travel that I had taken up with the man in the woods. I couldn't let Drew find out what had happened. I had to keep it a secret.

I opened the door to Josef's house, and Brayley flew into my arms. His warm embrace was comforting, but I knew I had left him without telling him.

"Where were you?" he asked, looking up at me. "I was scared. I thought something bad had happened to you."

"I'm okay," I said. "I just needed to get away."

"Did someone hurt you?" he asked.

I pulled away from him because I couldn't let him see the fear in my eyes. "Yes."

"What happened?"

"It doesn't matter. I'm fine now. Ward saved me," I said.

"Why didn't you come back? I could've helped."

"No," I said, shaking my head. "You didn't need to see me like that."

"Do you know who it was?" he asked.

I shook my head.

"Well, are you okay now?"

"I'm fine, Brayley. Enough about me," I said. "Are you okay? Josef didn't do anything to you, did he?"

"No," Brayley said. "Actually, Brother Josef's been gone. He told me yesterday he was going to see Mother, and he never came back."

"You've been here by yourself?"

"Well, Brother Daniel and Sister Celine have been here. Brother Daniel said Brother Josef will be back. He's just busy," Brayley said, smiling. "It's okay. I've been keeping myself busy."

"Doing what?"

"I found something," Brayley said, lowering his voice. "I think it's a basement."

"You've been snooping around his house?"

"It's what you do."

I gave him a look. "What did you find?"

Brayley shook his head. "I don't know, but you need to see it."

I followed Brayley into the empty kitchen. He opened the pantry door that was next to the cabinets revealing a dark entrance.

"I thought this was a pantry."

"Me too," Brayley said.

"Wait," I said, grabbing a lantern off of the counter. I moved past him and down the steps. The shutting of the door startled me, and I looked back to see Brayley holding a finger to his lips. I nodded and we continued down the steps. I stopped at the bottom. There were piles of junk that were stacked against the walls. My eyes scanned the rest of the room focusing my attention on the center of the room. The basement was dimly lit, but I could still make out the drawing of a five pointed star marked on the floor.

"Oh God."

"What is that?" Brayley whispered.

"I don't know," I said, stepping onto the hard cement basement floor. Brayley stayed on the step. He stared at the drawing.

I walked closer to it and knelt down. I touched the edges of the star. The light in the lantern began to flicker, and I stood up quickly.

"What?" he asked.

"I don't like this," I said.

"Me neither," Brayley said. "Let's go."

"Wait," I said, moving away from the symbol on the floor to a wooden table near the back wall. A book was laid open. I walked up to the book, and there were sketches of the five pointed star. I flipped the page. This time there was a photo of a young woman about my age. She was black, and her hair was pinned behind her head in a low bun. The bottom of the page was dated 1915. I turned the page again and gasped. It was a drawing of the woman who had attacked me. I knew it was her because the sketch had captured her matted hair and skeletal face. I didn't know whether to feel relieved that what I saw was real or terrified. On the top of the pages were thick black letters that etched the words FEED HER.

I could remember one evening my father had come home in a rushed manner. He had barged into the house and shut the door quickly. He had been out of breath from running.

We had rushed into the kitchen to see him with his back pressed against the door. He was breathing hard, and his eyes were wide with fright.

"What's wrong?" my mother had asked.

"Nothing," my father had said.

My mother had crossed her arms against her chest. "It doesn't seem like 'nothing.'"

My father glanced at us. "Kids, me and your mother need to talk."

"But-"

"Go," my father said firmly.

I never knew what it was they talked about, but I knew that day my father had seen something.

"October, we have to go," Brayley said. "I think I heard someone."

"Just one more minute," I said. I wanted to look away from the book, but I couldn't turn my eyes away from it. I turned to the next page, and there was a list of names written down in red ink. I turned the page, and the list of names continued. Some were familiar. I flipped to the next page, and I could recognize the Elders' names on it. Josef was written at the top. I scanned the list and froze once I got to the bottom.

My name was signed at the bottom of the list.

CHAPTER 26

"What does this all mean?" Zan asked.

We had gathered at Ward's cabin. We as in Zan, Nikki, Drew and I. It had been days after I had discovered the things inside Josef's basement. I hadn't told anyone at first instead choosing to dwell on it. I thought maybe if I took some time to think about it then it would all make sense, but I hadn't understood what it meant. When I told them what had happened to me, there was no denying it. They had all believed me. They didn't understand what was going on either. The only thing we were certain about was that there was no God in this place.

"There's something evil here," Ward said, leaning against the wall by the fireplace. He crossed his arms against his chest. "Josef always said we were chosen for something."

"Yeah, chosen for what?" Drew asked him.

Ward stared at Drew blankly. The tension was thick between the two of them so thick that Drew clenched his jaw whenever Ward looked at him. I placed my hand on top of Drew's turning his attention back to me. He looked at me, and his face softened. I could see Ward staring at us out of the corner of his eye, but I couldn't give him any attention. I didn't want Drew to get the wrong idea. Even if there was something unspoken between Ward and I.

"This just doesn't make sense. The worships, the Cleansings, the Annual Harvest," Nikki shook her head. "Who have we been praying to all this time?"

"You mean what have we been praying to," Ward corrected her.

"You said there was a photo of a woman?" Drew asked. "And she looked like you?"

I nodded. "The date on it was the date that Blue Corn was created."

"Could she have lived here at some point?" Drew asked.

"No," Zan said, shaking his head. "Everyone knows that October and her brother are…" He trailed off because we knew where he was going. Me and my brother were the first and only black people to live in Blue Corn.

"So if she didn't live here, what does she have to do with all this?" Nikki asked.

We were silent for a moment as we all considered this.

"There's something we're missing," Drew said, breaking the silence. "Something that Brother Josef isn't telling us about this place. How did Blue Corn really start?"

"Josef's great-great grandfather started this place," Nikki said.

"Yeah, but how?" I asked. "Renee said the outside world knows about us. How have we gotten away with being here undisturbed for a hundred years?"

There was a pause as we all stared at each other. This whole place was an illusion. A beautifully wrapped poison that we were all drinking. Some more willingly than others. But the beauty was starting to be peeled back revealing the ugly layers underneath.

The fire from the fireplace crackled, filling in the silence.

"This is all the more reason to leave," Zan said. "No one knows anything around here. For all we know, we could be worshipping the devil."

Ward snorted because Zan had a point.

"You're right. We need to get out of here, but when? Seeing Renee has Brother Josef on edge. Security around the fence is probably even tighter," Nikki said. "It won't be easy."

"Annual Harvest," I said.

Annual Harvest marked the beginning of spring, but that wasn't until a couple of weeks away. Annual Harvest was the perfect distraction. Everyone was required to attend which meant that there would be no security at the fence. It was when escaping would be the easiest.

"It could work," Ward said, nodding.

"We just need a plan and a good one," Drew said. "Because if we're caught then-"

"We're dead," Nikki finished for him. She turned her attention to me. "Especially you."

It was almost curfew by the time Drew and I left. Nikki and Zan had said their goodbyes earlier. They hadn't said where they were going, but I could see the smile on Nikki's face. I didn't need to ask. By the way they held onto each other, I knew they had wanted time alone.

Drew grabbed my hand. "Ready? It's getting late."

Drew was right. It was already dark, and I was scared to be in the woods. At least I would have Drew to walk with me, but that still didn't ease my fears.

"Yeah," I said, glancing at Ward who was tending to his fire. "I'll be out in a second."

"It's almost curfew," Drew glanced over at Ward.

I squeezed his hand. "I won't take long. I promise."

Drew nodded. He walked out the door, shutting it on his way out, but I knew he would be waiting by the door and probably eavesdropping. I walked over to Ward who looked up from poking at the kindling.

"Not gone yet?" he asked without looking up.

"I just wanted to say thank you," I said. "You didn't have to help me, but you did. I wouldn't have made it without you."

Ward looked up from the fireplace. The fire played over his dark eyes beckoning me to come closer. "It was nothing really. Just glad I could help."

"It was everything," I said. "I don't know how I could repay you."

"You don't need to," Ward glanced at the door. "Have you told him?"

"No."

"Are you going to?"

I chewed on the bottom of my lip because I hadn't decided yet. If I really wanted this thing between Ward and I to be nothing, then I needed to tell Drew. I shouldn't keep things from him. But then I wasn't so sure. Was there something between Ward and I?

"Do you love him?" he asked. "He's a good guy."

I looked away from him. "I don't know."

Ward nodded and turned back to the fire. "Goodnight, October."

"Goodnight," I said, walking to the door. I looked back at him. He was tending to the fire, but I could see that he was watching me out of the corner of his eye. I opened the door stepping out into the night. Drew was waiting by the door with a lantern in one hand.

"Ready?" he asked.

"Not yet," I said, pulling him to the side of Ward's cabin.

"What's wrong?" he asked.

I bit my lip not knowing what reaction I would get, but knowing it needed to be done. "Ward is the one who saved me. In the cornfields."

Drew raised an eyebrow at me. "Why didn't you tell me?"

"I don't know," I said. "I didn't want you to think anything was going on between us. If Ward hadn't shown up when he did, there was no telling what would've happened to me. I was so scared, Drew." He must have seen the fear in my eyes because he pulled me closer. "I don't know why I was attacked, but I'm thankful he was there."

Drew nodded. "Me too."

"You're not mad?" I asked him.

Drew shook his head. "No. I just wish you would've told me. No more secrets, okay?"

"Okay," I said, looking up into his face. He bent down and kissed me. A bell in the distance rang signaling the ten minute mark until curfew.

"Shit," Drew said, pulling away from me. "We have to get back."

"I know," I said. Drew held up the lantern, grabbing my other hand as we began our walk back to the community. The darkness enclosed us giving way only to the lantern that Drew held in front of us. Behind me the night seemed to be just a step away. I looked back and I could see shadows behind me. The thought of the woman from the cornfields began to creep into my head. There was no one behind me, and there was no need to get alarmed.

"You're okay?" Drew asked, stopping.

I glanced at him to see that he was looking back at me. "I'm fine."

"You're sure?"

I gave him a tight lipped smile and nodded. We kept walking. I held on to Drew's hand tightly, scared to let go.

"October..."

I stopped at the sound of the whisper. I looked behind me, catching a glimpse of something moving behind the trees.

"October, what's wrong?" Drew asked, coming to stand beside me.

"It's her."

"Who?"

"You didn't hear that? Or see anything?" I asked.

Drew shook his head. "Hear what? See who?" I gawked at him. Drew stared at me before squinting his eyes to look between the trees. He shook his head. "October, I don't see anything. There's no one there. Let's just get back, okay?"

I pursed my lips. Drew shrugged his shoulders and kept walking forward. I followed him quietly not because my suspicions had been resolved but because I was too afraid to see what was behind me.

CHAPTER 27

When I went back to school, no one questioned me. Apparently the news had spread that I was too distraught over my mother to come to school, and because my circumstance was special, it had been decided that I wouldn't have to suffer any punishment. It was a relief that I wouldn't feel the wrath of Sister Jennifer although it suggested that the only reason that I was getting this special treatment was because I was Josef's new "daughter." I spent the day in quiet dread not even finding solace in the company of Drew and Nikki. When asked why I was so quiet, I blamed it on my mother's ordeal.

"Is something wrong?" Nikki had asked. "You don't seem like yourself."

"I'm fine."

"Okay," she said, nodding. "I'm here for you."

"Thanks."

Days went by and finally the nightmares about my attack had begun to go away. Things were changing.

Nikki and I spent more time with Drew and Zan, either at his dad's shop or at the pond playing games that the adults in the community would disapprove of. The more time I spent with Zan, the more secrets he told, the more Nikki and I trusted him. Zan talked a great deal and pretty soon my ears became accustomed to the sound of his voice. Nikki seemed to have fallen in love, pleased by his attention to her. She laughed at his jokes and made every excuse to be nearer to him.

"When we leave here what is the first thing you're going to do?" Drew asked. We were sitting near the pond. Nikki and Zan were playing in the water splashing each other.

"Breathe," I said.

"You think it's going to be different?" he asked.

"I know it is. What about you?"

Drew thought about this. "I don't know." His voice was gentle. He held his palm up for me to grab, and I placed my hand in his. "But I'm ready."

It wasn't long before my tryst with Drew was discovered.

Genevieve seemed to be waiting on us one afternoon. Drew and I walked out of the schoolhouse paying attention to each other not noticing her at first until she stood in our path. Her arms crossed against her chest. She narrowed her eyes at us.

"So you're still together, huh?" she asked.

"What are you talking about, Genevieve?" I asked her.

Genevieve rolled her eyes. "Don't play dumb. Uncle's punishment didn't faze you, did it? As long as it wasn't you. You're such a good friend."

I took a step towards her, making her step back. Drew grabbed my arm.

"October…" he warned me.

"You don't know what you're talking about," I said to her.

Genevieve shrugged her shoulders. "Maybe I do. Maybe I don't. Maybe I thought that you would be into more loners, particularly ones who live in the woods."

I stiffened. She was referring to Ward. "What are you talking about?"

"Oh, I don't know," Genevieve said and smiled slyly. "Brother Ward is kinda cute, don't you think?"

I glanced at Drew. I could tell that he was uncomfortable with what Genevieve was saying because he wouldn't look at me.

"Genevieve, please," Drew said. "We have worship in a few and we're trying to get home."

"Then go," Genevieve snapped. "I'm not holding you up. I was just having a friendly conversation. No need to be so defensive." She sneered at me and walked past us, stopping beside me. She whispered into my ear. "Enjoy him while it lasts because pretty soon all of this won't even matter." She chuckled and walked away.

Before I could even think to wonder how Genevieve knew about Ward and I, the tension in the air was a hint that this conversation wasn't over.

"What was she talking about?" Drew asked.

I looked down at his hand still holding on to my arm. He wasn't going to let me go. "I don't know."

Drew raised an eyebrow. "You don't?"

I looked up at him. "No."

"You and him have been getting close," Drew said.

"He knew my father."

"We all did."

I stared at him because I was afraid this was going to happen. "Drew, it isn't like that. Ward is a friend."

"Fine," Drew said, moving his hand off my arm. He started to walk away. I grabbed his hand to stop him.

"Wait," I said. "Please."

Drew was reluctant, but he turned to me.

"There's nothing happening between me and him."

"I've never doubted this between us."

"Me neither, but I also never thought we would be together," I said to him.

"Well, we are," Drew said. "I want you, October. Only you. Can you say the same about me?"

"Yes," I said firmly. I could feel the stirring in my heart, and I pulled him closer to me. "I want you. I promise. There's no one else."

Drew nodded. "Okay."

I placed my hand on his cheek. He leaned down and kissed me. The taste of him was exhilarating, but the thought of Ward was in the back of my mind.

***

"Drew is a good guy," my father stated.

I looked over at him. I sat with my back against the barn wall beside my father. I had needed to see him. What Genevieve had said had stuck with me, and I wanted to ask my father about it. Maybe it was nothing, but there was a feeling that it meant something.

"I know he is."

"Then what's the problem?"

I shook my head. "Nothing."

"This isn't about Ward, is it?"

There was an awkward silence.

"You've been seeing him?" my father asked.

"He was the one who rescued me when I was attacked in the cornfields. He saved me," I said.

"And you should thank him and keep it moving."

"What do you have against him?"

"Nothing," he said quickly. "Is that why you came here? To talk about boys because-"

"No," I said. "I'm confused."

"About?"

"Father, none of this makes sense. I found something in Josef's basement. It was something evil. I don't know. There was this symbol-"

"I know," my father said, interrupting me.

"You know?" I asked. My father nodded. He looked down at the ground to avoid my gaze. "Does any of this have something to do with me? Something to do with why I'm here? Brother Daniel won't tell me. I can't ask Mother, and no one else seems to know."

"They know," my father said grimly.

"About what? What's the big secret?"

"October-"

"No," I said, cutting him off. "I want to know the truth. Genevieve said something about me enjoying my time while it lasts, what does that mean?"

"October, there's something I have to tell you," my father said, placing a hand over mine. "It's about Blue Corn. This place. It's not what you think it is."

"What is it?"

My father sighed. "Josef's great-great grandfather, William Walsh, founded this place a long time ago. It was back when the outside world was doing really bad. There was famine. Extreme famine. William Walsh couldn't stand the thought of being in a famine, so he made a deal with an old priestess. She promised him riches and land which he took and made into the farm. But there was a price," I leaned forward listening intently. "In exchange for the riches, William Walsh promised to worship her and never to leave this farm. The god that Josef makes us worship...it's a woman. The old priestess. Some say she's a witch. Whatever she is, she's still alive, and she lives in the woods. Haunting this place, reminding Josef of the deal William Walsh made."

I furrowed my eyebrows together confused. "What does this have to do with me?"

"The truth," My father shook his head. He closed his eyes and took a deep breath. "The truth is that you were brought here for a reason."

"Yeah, I know that part. But why?"

Father pinched the bridge of his nose, keeping his eyes shut. Whatever it was, I could tell he didn't want to say it, but I needed to know. "At the time, no one knew what William Walsh had done to build this place, but once the Elders found out, they were angry. The Elders wanted to be free of the witch's curse. But there was only one way."

"Which is?"

"The only way for Blue Corn to be free from the curse is to present the witch with a sacrifice. A young girl about her age," my father swallowed. "And one who looks like her. Once she is back in human form, she will grant our freedom, and the curse will be broken. It's you, October. You were brought here to be the sacrifice. She wants to be resurrected through you."

My jaw dropped. "What?"

"They want you," my father said. "That's why Josef won't kill you. He needs you alive."

"No," I said, shaking my head. I got up from the ground.

"October, wait," my father said. "I wasn't going to let that happen to you. Me and your mother promised that I would get you out by then."

"You could've said something."

"No," my father said, shaking his head. "I couldn't. You would've freaked out. It was the community's secret. October, you have to understand. If Josef knows that you know, then it's over for you. They'll keep you hidden until it's time. I didn't tell you because I was protecting you."

I gawked at him disgusted by everything all of a sudden. I turned my back on him and headed to the barn doors.

"October, wait!"

I could hear him calling my name, beckoning me to come back to him and apologizing for it all, but I ignored him. I didn't want an apology. I just wanted to get out of this place.

CHAPTER 28

I leaned over my bathroom sink and heaved. I gripped the edges of the sink to keep me steady as I threw up. When I was done, I turned on the faucet and ran water over the sink. I put my hands under the cold water and splashed water over my face.

I looked back up at my reflection. My eyes were red from lack of sleep, and my face was puffy. After learning the truth from my father, I had been transformed. I had been told my purpose and the strangeness about it was that it all had made sense. I didn't know why I had expected anything less. The signs had been pointing to the truth all along. A truth I had been trying to deny, but I didn't have to deny it any longer. The puzzle had been completed. Every moment that I had experienced here was connected, and it all pieced together a final photo.

I had prayed the nightmares would come easy like the sweetness of a sleep filled death. But my father's words replayed over in my head and I knew the nightmare would be brutal and harsh. I could feel the heat rise in my throat. My skin was hot and itchy. My body was on display for them all to witness the birth of a new season, and my death would bring the ultimate harvest. Their freedom. My arms stretched out to the sun. My fingers dripped blood and fed their tangible glory. Cloth and flesh and the smell of fire as I became the thing that I was meant to be. Their sacrificial lamb.

I felt like the ill-fated hero. The one who had been looking for their purpose only to discover that they were doomed and they could do nothing about it. It was their destiny, and their end had been prophesied long before their miraculous birth.

My knees were weak. I buckled underneath the weight and fear that I was feeling. I dropped down to the floor, resting my head between my knees. I took a deep breath.

"October? What's wrong?" a small voice called from behind the door. I didn't even bother to look up. I wasn't in the mood to talk. I just wanted to be alone.

"Just leave me alone."

"That's not going to happen."

I knew he would find me soon. I hadn't been out of my room in a whole day instead choosing to lock myself in here as some form of safety, closing my curtains from the threat of the others. For the first time, the danger that I felt from this community finally felt valid. I wanted this isolation from them because it mirrored the loneliness of death, and I hadn't wanted to feel anything or see anyone.

"You haven't been out of your room all day. You missed school. What's wrong?" Brayley's voice sounded like a sweet forgotten relic. I missed him, but I couldn't let him see me like this.

"It's me," I said softly. "They want me. Not you."

"What are you talking about?" Brayley asked from outside the door.

"It's me," I repeated with the same softness.

The doorknob began to twist. I could hear him fighting to get inside, but he wouldn't be able to. I had made sure of that.

"October, can you come out?" Brayley asked, continuing to twist the doorknob. "You're scaring me."

"It's me," I kept repeating it over and over. It felt like I said those words maybe a thousand times to myself. I had been wrong. This place had been built with a different seed than I could ever imagine. I had known this place was bad, but I hadn't imagined this.

Brayley was silent on the other end which meant he was still listening to me or he had left. I wrapped my arms around my knees and pulled them tighter against me. My stomach still lurched, but my breathing had slowed.

I could remember walking to the Plaza with my parents at a young age. I could remember the looks that the others gave me. They all stared at us. At the man holding hands with a small dark child and the embrace of a small baby in the hands of a pale mother. Anyone would have thought that the reason for their stares were so obvious. No one would have guessed the reason behind their stares had anything to do with the truth. But it was there then in their eyes and the way they looked at me. They knew a secret that I didn't. Their stares were all knowing like the watchful eyes of God.

"I wonder if she will ever find out," I could imagine they whispered about me.

How could I have not known? For so long, I had thought this was all about Brayley. That he had been at the center of it all, but I had been tricked. I should have known. Brayley was just collateral. He hadn't needed to be involved with this. He could have had a normal childhood if it wasn't for me. He didn't deserve any of this.

I got up from the floor and opened the bathroom door. My room was empty.

"Brayley?" I called out to him. My bedroom door was cracked, signaling Brayley had left. I walked over to the door and shut it, leaning my head against the door. I fumbled to feel the lock, and once I did, I locked it.

Suddenly, the doorknob to my bedroom began to turn. It twisted underneath my grip. I held on to it for a second before stepping back from the door.

"Brayley, I want to be alone."

"October?" Nikki's voice called from the other side.

I opened my mouth to answer, but I was interrupted by another voice that called to me.

"October? It's us," Drew's voice beckoned me to the door like a siren song, but I wouldn't fall into its trance. I stood frozen. Maybe if they couldn't hear me then they would decide to go away. "Please open the door."

"October, we can help. What's wrong?" Nikki asked. "What happened?"

I bit my lip, not wanting to say it out loud. I wanted Nikki to know, but I didn't want to put the truth out in the open. In the open, I wouldn't be able to take it back.

"October-"

"I know the truth," I said, cutting her off. They were silent. I thought for a second that they had left, but then Drew's voice came again.

"About what?"

"Why I'm here," I said. "The harvest that Josef's been talking about. It's me. He's going to sacrifice me in order for the rest of them to be free. That's why I was brought here."

"What are you talking about October?" Drew asked.

The door knob turned once more.

"October, let us inside," Drew said firmly.

"Did you know?" I asked.

"No," Nikki said. "October, I'm your bestfriend. I would never keep something like that from you. If I knew, I would have told you."

I believed her. It was him that I was directing the question towards.

"Drew, did you know?"

There was a pause. I held my breath and waited for the answer.

"October, I didn't know," he finally said. "I promise. Please. Let us in."

I walked towards the door, turned the lock, but I didn't open the door. It finally creaked open, and I stepped back. Drew walked in. I looked away from him.

"I didn't know," he pleaded. I looked back at him. The look in his eyes was so honest and was the only reason that I believed him.

Nikki appeared behind him. "You know I wouldn't keep anything like that from you."

I nodded my head, and before I could think, the tears flowed down my cheeks, and my knees buckled again.

"I got you," I could hear Drew say right before I started to fall to the ground. He caught me. I buried my face into his chest as he held me in his arms. "I got you," he said again softly.

"No one is going to sacrifice you," Nikki whispered to me as she rubbed my back.

CHAPTER 29

"*S*hould we tell her?" *I could remember the whispers coming from my parents' room. I would stand by the side of their door listening to them. "She would understand."*

At the time I didn't understand what they were whispering about. I knew it had to be something about me, but I wouldn't have guessed it would be as horrific as what the truth was.

"Would you?" my father had asked. Silence. "Then we wait. She'll know when she knows. And when she knows-"

"It's going to have to be you," my mother said, interrupting him. "You'll protect her. You always have."

Shortly after being told the truth, the announcement came. In three days, we would be having the Annual Harvest. In three days, I would be sacrificed for the greater good.

"Do you think he's joking?" Brayley asked, sitting beside me. He stared at the radio on my dresser.

I shook my head. "No." I grabbed the radio and threw it against the wall. It hit the wall with a crash and landed on the floor. Brayley stared at the radio stricken with silence.

"What are you going to do?" Brayley asked, breaking the silence.

"I need to talk to him," I said to Brayey. "I need some more time."

"What are you going to say?" Brayley asked.

"I don't know," I said. I didn't know what I would say to him, but I knew I couldn't let him win.

I headed out of my room and out into the hall. I looked over the banister to see Josef leading the Elders out of the kitchen and to the front door. I headed down the staircase just as Brother Daniel walked out of the kitchen. He crossed over to the staircase and stood at the bottom, watching Josef escort the Elders out of the door. I went to walk past him, but he stepped in front of me blocking my way.

"I need to talk to him," I said to Brother Daniel.

"No," he said, lowering his voice. "You need to stay under the radar."

"Does it matter? He's going to kill me anyway."

"You don't know what you're talking about."

"I know everything," I said, making Brother Daniel turn to look at me. "The reason I'm here. My purpose. My father told me."

Brother Daniel sighed at the mention of my father. He nodded once. "He's right."

"Well then, I need a plan."

"Plan about what?" a voice chimed in behind Brother Daniel. His eyes went wide, and he turned to see Josef standing behind him.

"Brother Josef-"

"Plan about what?" Josef repeated himself. He narrowed his eyes at me. He turned his attention to Brother Daniel. "Danny-"

"Plan about getting my mother awake," I said, getting his attention away from Brother Daniel.

Josef raised an eyebrow at me. "And how do you expect to do that?"

"I'll figure it out," I said to him.

"I bet you will," Josef said, turning to Brother Daniel. "We need to talk about Harvest."

"What about Harvest? Something wrong?" I asked.

Josef eyed me. "Nothing you need to know about."

"You sure about that?"

"What are you trying to say?" Josef asked, stepping towards me.

"Who are you going to kill this time?" I asked him. Josef scoffed but didn't answer. "I wish my mother could see you now. She would be disappointed."

Josef opened his mouth in silent shock. He clenched his jaw. "And I wish your father could see you. Hopefully you won't end up the same way he did."

I glared at him.

"Don't you ever think that you are untouchable, October."

"You aren't either," I muttered.

Josef stepped towards me in a menacing way. Brother Daniel stepped quickly in between us. "You needed to talk?"

Josef glared at me but nodded. He turned and headed towards the living room. Brother Daniel followed. He looked back at me and shook his head disapprovingly. I watched him disappear into the living room.

"What did he say?" Brayley asked. I looked up the stairs to see him standing over the banister.

I shook my head. Brayley sighed. I walked back up the stairs and went to stand beside him. "Don't worry. I'll figure it out."

***

When the clock struck midnight, I crawled out of bed with my shoes already on. I pulled off my nightgown, which was covering my dress. I grabbed my coat and headed towards my door. I opened it and peered out into the dark hall. I tiptoed out of my room and pulled the door closed. I made my way to the staircase and tiptoed down them as quietly as I could. I stopped at the end of the stairs and listened to any stirring coming from upstairs, signaling that someone had heard me. There was nothing.

I kept tiptoeing through the foyer until I was out of the door and standing on the porch. I stood there for a second taking in the glow that was radiating from the moon. It cast a purplish black tint on the ground. I held my breath and made a run for it. I kept running until I reached the side of the church where I stopped to catch my breath.

Suddenly, a hand slid over my mouth and over my waist pulling me tightly against them. Before I could yell, a voice whispered into my ear to be quiet, and I stopped fighting. It was Ward. I looked back to see him holding a finger to his lips. I raised an eyebrow, and that's when he mouthed the word Guard. I nodded just as we heard movement to the left of us. I stepped back pressing myself into Ward. I could feel his hard body underneath my hands. He stiffened.

We watched as a Guard moved a flashlight beam over the backyard of the church looking for people who were disobeying the curfew. We waited until he walked over to the stage before we moved back to the front of the church. As soon as we saw him move away from the church, we took off running for the cornfields. I stopped once we got deep into the rows to catch my breath.

"I didn't mean to-"

"It's fine," Ward said, cutting me off before I could finish. His face was flushed. I didn't know whether it was because of the run or because of me. "Let's just keep going, okay?"

I nodded, and we kept going. I pushed through the hard leaves. The bushels were as stiff as cold bodies. Once we made it to the end of the field, I knelt down. Ward knelt down beside me.

I watched as the Guard standing by the entrance to the fence looked down at the radio in his hand as it clicked on. He moved the radio to his ear to listen to the receiving voice. Whatever the voice had said, the Guard nodded and walked away from the entrance. Once he was out of sight, I peered out of the bushels of corn. There weren't any other Guards around.

"Let's go," I said to Ward. He nodded, and I ran to the fence with him close behind. I could hear his breath behind me as he kept up with me.

When I got to the fence, I grabbed the metal bars. "Renee?" I called out to her. No answer. I needed her to be here. We didn't have much time.

"What if she isn't here?" Ward asked.

"She has to be," I said, lowering my voice. "Renee?"

Ward placed a hand on my shoulder. "They might have spotted her-"

"October?" a voice called from the darkness. Renee suddenly appeared behind the fence. When she saw me, her eyes lit up. She smiled, but then her attention went to Ward. "Who is this?"

"A friend," I said to her.

She nodded at him. She turned her attention back to me. "I'm glad you made it. I didn't think you would."

"A promise is a promise," I said to her. "Is our promise still on?"

"Of course," she said. She stepped closer to the fence. "I'm not going to leave you."

We stared at each other for a second as I thought about everything I missed not being with her. "I think Josef might be on to us."

"Well you best get out of there," she said, rattling the bars. "Can you get out of there?"

"We're gonna have to climb," Ward said. "Help each other up."

"That means one of you is going to have to stay," Renee said.

"No," I said firmly. "I'm not going to let that happen."

"She's right," Ward said. "Someone's going to have to stay."

"I'm not letting any of you stay."

"October-" Renee started.

"It's either no one or all of us," I said, cutting her off. "I'm not leaving anyone."

She opened her mouth to object but stopped. She nodded in understanding. "Okay."

"We have a plan," Ward said to her. "We're going to escape during our Annual Harvest. It's in two days."

Renee nodded at Ward. She looked at me and held out her hand through a slit between the bars. I took it. "Two days," she said.

I nodded. "Two days."

She squeezed my hand in reassurance before letting go.

"Come on," Ward said, getting my attention.

I nodded. I looked back at Renee, and she gave me a small smile. I smiled back before turning to follow Ward back into the cornfields.

"Where are you going?" Ward asked, stopping me as I started to walk off from him.

"I can make it," I said.

Ward placed a hand on my arm to stop me. "You won't. You can stay with me for the night."

"You sure?" I asked him. He avoided my gaze but nodded.

"Yeah, my cabin isn't far," he said.

I was unsure about this. Not because I didn't trust Ward but because I didn't trust myself. I agreed anyway and figured it wouldn't hurt if I stayed the night. I would leave first thing in the morning.

I followed Ward to his cabin. We walked in, and I noticed how comforting it felt. Ward brought me a blanket and then turned to go to his room.

"Ward?" I asked. He stopped but didn't turn around. "Could you stay with me? For a little while."

He turned slightly. He hesitated for a second and then came and sat next to me on the couch. I draped the blanket over me.

"You think we can pull this off?" I asked him.

Ward rubbed his hand through his hair. "I don't know, but once it's done, there's no turning back." I nodded in understanding. "People are going to get hurt. People that you care about."

"Like you?"

"Like Drew," Ward said. "I get it. You two are good for each other. He brings out the best in you because...well, he is the best. You both care about people. People see you." Ward tore his eyes away from mine.

"I see you."

I laid my hand in the space between us. Ward went from avoiding my gaze to staring at my hand. I slid my hand closer to him. He closed his eyes, and after what felt like a small eternity, he slid his hand over mine.

I shouldn't be doing this, I thought. *Think about Drew.*

I moved closer to him.

"October," he whispered. He was warning me to think about what I was doing.

But it was too late.

I touched my forehead against his. I placed my hand on the back of his neck pulling his lips to mine. I kissed him. He kissed back. Hesitant at first. Then faster and longer. He pulled me closer until I was straddling him. Suddenly, he stopped.

"No," he said sharply. "We can't."

"Well, we just did," I said, catching my breath.

"We can't, October."

I sighed and moved off of him. "I know. Drew-"

"It's not about Drew," Ward said, cutting me off. His cheeks turned rosy. He took in a ragged breath.

"Then what is it?"

Ward swallowed. At first I was confused, but then he looked at me and there was something in his eyes. I knew what he was about to say even before he said it.

"October, I'm your brother."

CHAPTER 30

His words hung in the air. I stared down at the floor not wanting to look at him. I couldn't believe what he had just said.

"October?" he said. Ward and I had kissed. More like I had kissed him and he had let me. Not only did I go behind Drew's back but it backfired on me.

"How?" I asked him.

"Brother Dennis is my father," Ward said.

I gasped and looked up at him. "He's yours?"

"October, no," Ward reached out to touch my arm. I moved away from his touch, getting up from the couch. I didn't want to look at him let alone touch him. "He's just as much yours as he is mine. Even more so yours."

"I have to go," I said, grabbing my jacket off the arm of the couch.

"October, wait," he said. "I can explain."

I shook my head. "Why would you let me do that?"

Ward was lost for words. "I'm sorry," he said, fumbling for his words. "But I wanted it to happen."

"Oh God," I said, moving to the door. I couldn't be here. I had to leave. I grabbed the doorknob, opening the door. A hand pressed itself against the door, shutting it. "Ward, please," I said, not turning around. "I have to go." I heard him sigh. He dropped his hand from the door. I opened it and left.

Once outside, I stopped on the porch. I grabbed the railing and steadied myself. My hands were shaking. I didn't want to believe that Ward was my father's child, but it was starting to make sense. The tension between him and my father. The unspoken bond. It had always been there. I just hadn't been able to see it.

I ran home. I didn't even care that I was running in the woods at night by myself. I just wanted to get home. Once I was inside of the house, I ran up the staircase but stopped at the sound of moaning. It was coming from upstairs.

I moved up the staircase slowly, and the moaning grew louder. It sounded as if it was coming from Josef and my mother's bedroom. I paused once I was at the top of the staircase and realized that their bedroom door was slightly ajar. I stopped at the side of the door. I held my breath and peered inside. My eyes grew wide at the sight of Genevieve on top of Josef as he thrust himself inside of her. Her face was contorted in painful pleasure. I gasped loudly, making them freeze. They looked at the door, and I moved back, pressing my back against the wall. I covered my mouth with my hand to keep them from hearing me.

"What was that?" I could hear Josef asking. There was a pause.

"It's nothing Josef," Genevieve said. There was another pause, this time longer. I could hear Genevieve giggle. I closed my eyes and screamed inside as I waited for it to be over.

CHAPTER 31

I stared at the pulpit as Josef preached about Sinners and Saints. I looked over at the Sinners side at Nikki and her family. She looked at me and smiled. I couldn't let her see how distressed I was. I didn't need her asking questions, so I looked away.

The image of Genevieve and Josef replayed over in my mind. I couldn't believe what I had seen. Josef and Genevieve were together. I took a long shaky deep breath. I wondered if Josef was forcing Genevieve to be with him, but by the look of it, she hadn't seemed too sad about it.

Brayley's hand found mine. I looked at him, and he mouthed the words "you okay." I nodded, but I knew Brayley could tell that I wasn't. He narrowed his eyes at me but turned his attention back to Josef.

"October?"

I looked at Josef to see that he was staring at me. The congregation had grown quiet. I looked around to see that the others were looking at me. I looked back at Josef, who beckoned me to come forward.

"Would you like to lead us in a prayer for your mother?" he asked.

My mouth grew dry. My heart raced. I could feel everyone's eyes on me, but I couldn't move. I shook my head.

"Oh, come on. Don't be scared," he said. "We're all family here."

I stared at him as I saw a glint of light in his eyes. He was doing this on purpose. Had he seen me looking at him and Genevieve?

I stood up. My mother didn't need prayer. She needed to get away from Josef. I could feel the tears forming in my eyes, and I knew that I had to get out of there. The next thing I knew I was running out the door. I could hear the gasps behind me, but I kept running. I stopped at the side of the church. The cool air filled my lungs as I gulped it down.

I heard a rustling in the distance. I looked to see that it was Ward tending to the cemetery. He saw that it was me and froze. My face grew hot. I walked away towards the back of the church before he could say anything. I was embarrassed. When I looked at him, all I could see was the kiss.

I walked to the stage and climbed on top of it. I went to stand in front of the microphone. I looked out at the empty backyard and imagined myself as the prophet. What would I have done differently?

"You okay?" a voice asked, waking me from my daze. Drew was walking towards me.

"What are you doing here?" I asked him.

Drew smirked. "I asked you first."

"I just needed to get out of there," I muttered. I watched as he climbed onto the stage and stood in front of me. He grabbed my hands.

"Would you like to come to my place?" he asked. "I'm cooking. It's been awhile since we've had company. My father would love to have you over and-"

"You don't have to convince me," I said, smiling. "I would love to come."

Drew smiled. "Good. I'm making dessert too."

"Cookies?"

"Apple pie," Drew noticed the expression on my face. "Cookies it is."

I laughed. He smiled and leaned closer. The gap between us lessened as our noses touched. I closed my eyes and breathed him in. I was starting to love him.

***

The smell of chocolate greeted me once the Keegan's front door opened. It was Brother Peter. He gave me a small smile.

"Hi, October," he said. "Come in."

"Hello, Brother Peter," I said as I stepped into the house. This was my first time in their house, and I was surprised at how clean it was. Colorful flowers stood in the corners of the room.

"It's been awhile since we've had company," he said, moving down the hall. I followed him into the kitchen to see Drew taking a pan out of the stove. He looked back at us.

"Hey," he said, smiling.

I smiled back. I tried not to blush too hard since his father was standing next to me.

Brother Peter cleared his throat. "Let me know when it's ready, Drew.'"

"Yes, Father," Drew said. Brother Peter left us. Drew looked at me and smiled again. I walked over to him. I noticed the pan that he had pulled out of the stove was filled with freshly baked chocolate chip cookies. He grabbed one off of the pan and broke it in two, handing one of the pieces to me.

I took it and bit into it. It was warm and melted in my mouth. Drew chuckled.

"What?" I asked.

"You have something on your lip," he said. He reached and wiped my bottom lip with his finger. He placed his finger in his mouth and sucked the chocolate off. I tried not to stare as he looked back at me.

"What did you cook?" I asked, trying to direct both of our attention somewhere else.

"Corn casserole," he said. "It was my mother's favorite."

"You never talk about your mother."

Drew shrugged. He opened the cupboard and pulled out three glasses. "She loved it here. She said she loved being part of a big family." Drew stared down at the counter. For once, I saw something different in his eyes, and it wasn't hope.

I moved closer to him. I placed a hand on his shoulder. He looked up at me and stared. It was like he was looking at me, but he wasn't.

"I'm sorry, Drew," I said. "What Josef did to your mother was wrong."

"I know."

He placed a hand on the side of my face. He moved closer, touching his forehead to mine. I wanted to tell him that I had kissed Ward. I wanted to tell him that I had liked it. I wanted to tell him what I saw between Josef and Genevieve, but I couldn't. He leaned closer, brushing his lips against mine waiting for me.

"Not now," I whispered, pulling away.

Someone cleared their throat at the doorway, and we looked over to see Brother Peter walking by. Drew chuckled and went back to preparing the drinks. I bit my lip wanting more.

"Do you want any help?" I asked.

"You know how to cook?" he asked.

I picked up the pan of cookies quickly avoiding his question. "I'll take these to the table."

Drew laughed and nodded.

I walked into the dining room, placing the cookies at the table. There were only three chairs at the table. In the middle of the table was a vase filled with one red rose. I touched one of the petals to feel how soft it was.

It had been a couple of days after the Annual Harvest.

I remembered because my father had insisted that we go over and show our sympathy even though her death was supposed to be celebrated.

"Should we be doing this?" I had asked him.

"Yes," my father had said, knocking on the door. "We should."

Drew had opened the door. I remembered his eyes. They were bloodshot from crying.

My father handed Drew a bouquet of flowers that my mother had made. "We're sorry about your loss."

Drew took the flowers. He had looked at me. I stared at him, and that's when I heard the music. The sound of a piano playing. Drew had looked back into the house.

"Thank you," he mumbled and closed the door.

I recognized the music as it poured into the dining room. I went to stand by the door to see Brother Peter sitting at the piano that was in the middle of the living room. As he was playing, he sang softly. Sitting on top of the piano was a photo of Drew's mother.

"He plays a song for her everyday," Drew's voice whispered into my ear.

"Now I know where you got your talent from," I said, looking back at him. He stared at me, chewing on his lip. He moved away from me and walked into the dining room. He placed the food on the table.

"Hungry?" he asked.

I smiled.

***

I left a little after dinner before it got too dark. I closed the door softly so that no one would hear me. I walked into the kitchen to find Brother Daniel standing by the sink fixing him a drink of water.

"Brother Daniel?"

He looked back at me. "Call me Danny. I think we're passed formalities."

I nodded at him. "We need to talk."

Danny took a sip of water before answering. "About what?"

"About our escape. I need a favor."

Danny raised an eyebrow. "What is it?"

"At the Annual Harvest, I'm going to need your help."

Danny pursed his lips hesitantly. "October, you know I can't do that."

I stepped towards him. "Please."

Danny shook his head. "I'll see what I can do, but I can't make any promises."

I nodded. "Thank you." I was about to walk out of the kitchen when Danny stopped me.

"We're even now," he said to me.

I nodded in understanding.

CHAPTER 32

We all stood watching the stage as Josef performed one of his miracle works. A young girl who had been sick was getting healed. Josef had his eyes closed mumbling prayers with his hand pressed against the young girl's forehead. Some people watched in silent worry. Others had their eyes closed mumbling prayers along with him.

I could remember Josef performing a miracle on Brayley as a child. Brayley had gotten really sick. My parents had thought he wasn't going to make it. He had lost a lot of weight, and he could barely walk.

My mother carried his lethargic body in her arms. He stared up at the sky and I noticed that his eyes had lost their brightness. His skin looked so ashened.

Josef had taken Brayley into his arms and fed him a clear liquid.

After a couple of minutes, Brayley stirred in his arms. He sat up and reached not for our mother. But for me.

Eight year old me hadn't understood then. I grabbed my father's hand and withdrew from him. I didn't understand why he had reached for me.

"Cover for me?" I whispered to Nikki, who was silently playing to herself with her eyes closed. She nodded in response without opening her eyes.

I looked around me to see that even the Guards were mumbling prayers except Danny. His eyes were glued to the stage, but he looked more bored than moved. He caught my eye and nodded. I nodded back. I was on my way to see my father, and this was Danny's signal that the coast was clear.

I moved towards the back of the crowd. No one paid too much attention to me. I finally made it just as a hand grabbed my arm. I looked back to see that it was Genevieve.

"What do you want?" I asked her. I was trying my best to avoid her. Ever since I had caught her with Josef, I couldn't stand to look at her.

Genevieve glanced around to see if anyone was watching us.

"We need to talk," she said, pulling me away from the crowd near a tree where we stood behind it. "I saw you. The other night-"

"Genevieve, I don't care," I said, cutting her off. "Do whatever you want. With whoever you want."

Genevieve scoffed. "It's not like that."

I crossed my arms against my chest. "Then what is it? Because to me, it looked like you liked it."

Genevieve looked down at the ground in embarrassment. She chewed on her lip. "It's not so bad. The guilty feeling goes away after a while."

"How long?"

"Ever since I could," she said.

"Does your mother know?"

Genevieve looked up at me. "I don't know, but I think so."

I was taken aback. What kind of mother would allow something like that to happen to her child? I knew Sister Jennifer was cruel, but I didn't know she was just as evil as Josef.

"Why is he doing that to you?" I asked her.

Genevieve swallowed. "Your mother could never give him what he needed. Only what he wanted."

I furrowed my eyebrows together confused. "What does he need?"

"The thing he couldn't get from my mother," Genevieve said. "I was born and as you know girls can't be prophets."

"What are you saying?"

"I'm saying that it's my turn now," Genevieve gave me a small smile. "I can give him what he needs." Genevieve placed a hand on her stomach. "A true heir."

I thought I was going to be sick. I backed away from her. "Genevieve, that's sick. He's your uncle."

"And father," Genevieve said. "My mother said we have to keep it in the family. It's always been that way."

"Oh my God," I whispered under my breath.

"It keeps me safe," Genevieve said. I could see the hurt in her eyes. Maybe it had been there all this time.

"You don't have to do it."

Genevieve snorted. She shook her head as tears appeared in her eyes. "You know you're the only person who thinks that." Genevieve wiped her tears on the backs of her hands. "That's the reason he's afraid of you. He told me that once. You could take this whole place away from him and everyone would follow."

"That's not true," I said. "They love him. They made their choice to follow him."

"Why not you then?" she asked.

I raised my eyebrow at her. "What do you mean?"

"They made a choice to follow him when clearly you're the one who can save them," Genevieve said. "I know you have the key."

"I don't know what you're talking about," I said, shaking my head. "I don't have the key."

Genevieve stepped towards me. We were so close I could feel her breath on my face. "Do whatever you want with it. I don't care. Just do what you have to do and leave."

"Leave?" I asked her. "That's not possible."

"Of course it's possible," she said. "Why do you think Josef wants his key back?"

I didn't answer partly because I couldn't let her think I had the key and partly because I didn't know the answer to the question.

Genevieve smirked. "That key opens a lot of doors, October, including the fence."

My jaw dropped before I could try to hide my surprise.

"See?" she said to me. "I knew you had it." She walked away, but before she could get too far, I grabbed her arm to stop her.

"Are you going to tell?" I asked her.

"This was never your home to begin with," Genevieve said with a small smile. "I may hate you, but I don't want to see you die."

***

The barn was a short distance from the church, but it was a lonely walk. The night came fast, and my fear grew faster. The walk felt like torture as I looked back to see if anyone was following me. Out of habit, I placed my hand on my neck. My scar had healed, but my wounds were still there. I could feel a coldness on the back of my neck, and I froze. I knew it was her.

"I know it's you," I said aloud. "I can feel you. You can't get me though. I won't let you."

This time I could feel the coldness behind my ear.

"Harvest is upon you…" I could hear her whisper. It was as if her voice was blended into the air.

I took in a deep breath and kept walking. Finally, I made it to the barn where I stopped at the door to catch my breath. I placed my hand on the iron handle and opened the door.

My father appeared hiding behind a stack of hay.

"Hey," I said.

"Hey," he said, walking over to a lantern that sat on the ground. He picked it up. "How's your mother?"

"Not good," I said, watching him as he carried the handle of the lantern in his mouth and began to climb the ladder. "I came to talk to you."

I waited as he climbed up the ladder. He set the lantern down and looked over the railing. "About?"

I hesitated. "Ward."

"What about him?" my father asked. He raised an eyebrow at me questioningly.

"Who is he?" I asked him.

My father leaned against the railing and sighed. "Why?"

"Father, I need to know who he is," I said to him. "Please."

My father hesitated but finally responded, "He's my son, October."

I groaned because I didn't want it to be true. We had kissed. I had felt something, but how? He was almost like my brother in a weird way. "How?"

"It was before Lauren. I was young. It was a mistake. Sister Mary was married. She passed him off as her husband's, but we both knew it wasn't. No one could know. She could've been branded for that." My father clenched his jaw and sucked in his breath. "Leaving Ward is my biggest regret. But there isn't anything I can do about that now."

"What about acknowledging him?" I asked him. My father avoided my gaze. "Ward watched you raise us. We weren't even yours-"

"You are mine," my father snapped. "You and your brother will always be mine. You're my children."

"He's your child too. More so than us."

"October, it's complicated," he said.

"Well then, I know why we were drawn to each other," I said. My father narrowed his eyes at me, and for the first time, I saw him in a different light. "You know we kissed by the way. My own brother. I feel disgusted."

My father sighed. "I thought you were with Drew."

"That's not the point," I said sharply. "But I understand why we're so attracted to each other. We both know what it feels like to be abandoned."

My father went still. I turned on my heels to leave, stopping only at the sound of his voice.

"I'll see you in a couple of days," he said to me. Because in a couple of days the Annual Harvest would happen and we would make our escape. My father was probably planning to leave us again. "Be ready."

I realized then who my father was. He was always like this. Nothing else mattered to him but the outside. It was why he had left Ward and why he had chosen my brother and I.

I shook my head disappointingly and left the barn. Our connection was only ever about the outside. He didn't really love me.

CHAPTER 33

The next morning before I could walk into the schoolhouse, I was stopped on the steps. It was Ward. We hadn't spoken since the night we had kissed, but I knew I would have to say something to him eventually. Now he stood in front of me with a guilty look on his face.

"Can we talk?" Ward asked, shoving his hands inside his pockets.

"Okay."

I walked over to the side of the building so that no one would see us. Ward was silent as he followed me around the building.

"What do you want?" I asked, turning to him. I crossed my arms over my chest. Ward stared at me intensely. He knew I couldn't resist him like that. I shook my head and started to walk away. "No, I can't-"

"October, wait," Ward said, grabbing my arm. I closed my eyes and sighed. His touch made goosebumps crawl up my arms. "I'm sorry. I wanted to tell you who I was, but it didn't feel like it was ever the right time."

"Yeah, there were plenty of right times," I said. "You knew who I was to you and yet you let me kiss you." That kiss shouldn't have happened between us. If I had known who Ward was, then I wouldn't have done it. But he had known and that was the problem.

"I didn't know how to stop you. And it was too late. We had already felt it."

I grimaced at the idea of it. "I know."

Ward shook his head. "We can't feel like that towards each other, but we can't ignore each other either."

I avoided his gaze because he was right. The feeling of Ward's lips against mine made me tremble and feel sick at the same time. We couldn't have feelings for each other. That would be just wrong. But I couldn't not talk to him.

I looked back at him and nodded. "As much as I want to stay away from you, I can't. I need your help. We all do."

Ward nodded.

"Is everything okay?"

I looked over to see Drew standing at the corner of the schoolhouse watching us. I moved away from Ward. "I'm fine."

"You sure?" Drew asked, eyeing Ward. "This guy just keeps popping up."

Ward took a step towards him. "That's because I'm her brother."

"He's your what?" Drew asked, directing his attention to me.

"Drew..." I stepped towards him and placed my hand on his. "I didn't know."

Drew looked at Ward. "What do you want with her?"

Ward clenched his jaw. "I just wanted to talk."

Drew opened his mouth to retort, but I stopped him. "It's fine," I said. Drew stared at me, and I could tell he didn't want to let it go, but he nodded and turned back around the corner. I turned my attention back to Ward.

"Just help us get to the fence, okay? We'll figure out the rest."

Ward nodded. I gave him a small smile before walking back.

"I don't regret it," I could hear Ward mutter behind me.

I didn't look back at him, but if I did, I probably wouldn't have been able to turn back around.

***

After school, Nikki and I went to visit my mother.

"I kissed Ward," I said aloud.

"You what?" Nikki said, stopping in the road.

"I didn't mean to," Nikki gave me a look. "I mean I did but I shouldn't have."

"Well, why did you?" Nikki asked.

"I don't know," I said. "But I shouldn't have." I sighed. "There's something else."

Nikki raised an eyebrow at me. "What? Did you and him-"

"No," I said firmly. I swallowed. "Ward is my brother."

Nikki's eyes grew wide. "What? How?"

"My father," I said, shaking my head. "I wouldn't have kissed him if I knew."

Nikki looked almost disgusted. "Well, are you going to tell Drew?"

I shrugged. Nikki shook her head in disbelief. "Let's just get to the hospital."

Nikki nodded in agreement as if she wanted no more parts of our conversation.

When we got inside of the hospital, Josef was already standing by my mother's bed.

"What's wrong?" I asked. He didn't answer. I walked over to the other side of the bed and grabbed her hand. It was cold.

"Mother?" I called out to her. Her eyes were shut, and her head was leaned over to the side. "Mother?"

"She's not going to answer," Josef finally said. "She's gone."

I looked up at him. His hair was messy, and his eyes were bloodshot from crying.

"You did this," I said.

"What did you say?"

"Brother Josef?" a voice interrupted us. It was Brother Corbin. He had short dark hair that had begun to gray in spots and wore large glasses. He walked up to the bed.

"Is she dead?" I asked him.

"October, I'm really sorry," Brother Corbin said. "But she was really sick."

I glared at him. "She wasn't sick."

Josef cleared his throat. Brother Corbin blushed and lowered his head.

"I'm sorry for your loss, October. But your mother is in a much better place," Brother Corbin said. He gave me a small pity smile and left.

"I can't believe this," Josef mumbled under his breath.

I looked back at him. "This is your fault."

"I didn't mean for this to happen," Josef said, shaking his head. "I didn't know she would take so many."

"You didn't know?" I asked. "You knew what those pills would do to her!" Josef began to cry. "And now she's dead." I stared at her pale face. I placed my hand on her face and caressed her cheek. "You should've left us alone. We were fine without you. We all would be fine without you!"

Josef was taken aback. "Watch who you're talking to," Josef snarled. "You may be family, but there are still consequences for your actions."

"Let's get one thing clear," I said to him. "You and I will never be family."

CHAPTER 34

Eve tempted Adam, and they fell from grace, their souls died, and my soul with it. I mourned for my mother. Emptiness and heartbreak filled me. When I saw her lifeless body being carried away from the hospital and into the church, I couldn't believe it, but the funeral made everything feel real. I thought back to what she would've wanted me to remember about her. The memory of her was only as brilliant as her life. One day I would sleep beside her in that garden and rest with the other fallen souls.

Josef was the reason my mother was dead, and he knew it. He had cried out in the result of her death. It had always occurred to him that my mother was somewhat invincible and unmovable like an old tree, but Josef had finally realized the ramifications of his actions. It shocked him that my mother hadn't been able to weather the storm.

***

It was a pretty day.

The kind of day that my mother loved. Everything was just right. The blue in the sky. The white in the clouds. The slight breeze in the air that didn't make you cold but cooled you off.

Josef spoke over the casket. The sound of his voice boomed over us. His voice blanketed my mother's body as her casket was open for all of us to see her. I wondered what she thought of him speaking over her body and what she thought of us looking over her.

Beside me, Brayley's body shuddered, and I could think of no way to console him but to let him cry. Sometimes there was nothing else to do. I stared into the casket at my mother's still body. I hated the dress that Josef put on her. I had asked that she be dressed differently, but Josef wouldn't let me have a say in her arrangements.

"...May she rest in His peace..." he said.

"May she rest in His peace," the crowd mumbled back.

As Josef continued, I scanned the crowd.

That's when I saw her.

In the distance stood my mother's figure. Her image moved with the breeze. She waved at me. I glanced around to see if anyone was seeing what I was seeing, but everyone was either paying attention to Josef or looking inside my mother's casket.

"Remember that I was kind," my mother's voice took me away.

I watched as the sun shined brightly on her face as she smiled up at the sky. She wore a white dress. A dress that she would have been happy in. Her blonde hair blew in the wind.

"Are you happy now?" I had asked her.

She turned to me and placed her hand on my face. Her touch was warm like the sun. She smiled. "You'll be free too, my dear."

I looked back at the figure in the distance to see that she had been transformed. I gasped. It wasn't my mother anymore but of a young black woman. The woman from the photo that I found in Josef's basement. She looked innocent, but I knew differently. She was a monster on the inside.

"Drew, it's her," I whispered to him. He was standing on my other side. "She's here."

I had told the others what my father had told me. The truth about how Blue Corn was started. We all agreed that we had to leave before it was too late for me.

Drew's hand slipped into mine. "She's not going to hurt you," he whispered back, tracing the inside of my palms with his fingers. During Josef's eulogy, I noticed how his body had drawn nearer to me. His warmth brought me comfort.

I looked out into the distance to see that the figure of the woman was gone. I glanced at Ward who stood on the other side of my mother's casket. He looked at me. I looked away from him. I knew what he was thinking. We both knew our father would have wanted to be here.

After Josef's eulogy, I went and stood off to the side. Drew had wanted to stay with me, but I had asked to be alone. He had understood but reassured me that he wouldn't be far. I watched as Danny led a group of men as they lowered my mother's casket into the ground. He watched her casket with a pained expression on his face.

"How are you, October?"

I didn't have to look to see that it was Josef. I wondered if he even considered that he was the last person I wanted to see.

"My mother is dead," I said, setting my gaze on him. "How do you think I feel?"

Josef pursed his lips. I expected him to argue with me, but he ignored my curtness. "The Annual Harvest is tomorrow. Are you prepared?"

"I think I've paid my wages, don't you think?"

"I beg to differ."

"Excuse me?"

"I'm going to ask you something," Josef started. "It would be best if you answered the question as truthfully as you can. It might save your life."

I rolled my eyes. "What is it?"

"Do you have my key?"

"We're still on this?" I said to him. Josef raised an eyebrow at me. "No."

He narrowed his eyes at me. "You're lying."

I didn't respond to him.

"Have you figured it out yet?" Josef asked me. I furrowed my eyebrows together confused. "Have you figured out why you were chosen?"

I gawked at him. Yes, I had figured it out, but I didn't want to admit it. "No."

Josef nodded as if he knew that wasn't the truth either. "Well, I hope tomorrow gives you motivation to tell the truth.'"

I glared. "You know sacrificing me isn't going to set you free. You're going to hell for all the things you've done.'"

"I think I'll be just fine," Josef said, giving me a small smile. He turned to leave but stopped himself. He turned back and wiggled his finger at me. "But who says it's going to be just you?"

Now this surprised me. "Wait. What are you going to do?" I called out to him. He chuckled just as Brayley walked past him. Josef placed a hand on his shoulder stopping him. Brayley looked up at him.

"You okay?" Josef asked him. "Do you need anything?"

Brayley shook his head and gave me a weird look. He might not have known what was going on, but I did and Josef knew it.

"Good," Josef said, smirking behind Brayley's back. "After tomorrow, everything will be okay."

***

"It's not just me. He's going to kill Brayley too."

It was after the funeral. My mother's body had been laid to rest, and everyone had gone their separate ways. I laid in bed crying over my mother's death and crying that I might be the blame for Brayley's impending fate. Nikki sat on the bed beside me. She said she would stay by my side as long as I needed her. She was the best friend I could ever have, and she was more than I deserved.

"Why would he do that?" I asked, but once I asked the question out loud, I already knew the answer. Josef was trying to hurt me in the worst way. I had imagined what life would be like without friends, without the farm but never had I imagined life without Brayley.

"Did he say that?" Nikki asked.

"In so many words," I said. I could see that Nikki was twiddling her thumbs. "Are you sure you want to leave with me?"

"Yes."

"What about your family?" I asked her.

"They will understand," Nikki said. "They want me to do what's best for me."

"But if I leave, they'll be stuck here," I said to her. "Forever."

"I know."

"Can you live with that?"

Nikki sighed. "October, don't make this about me."

"But it's more than just about me," I said. "It's about all of us. You all are risking your lives for me. Why?"

"Because you're the only one who can save us," Nikki said.

I sighed at the burden of her statement. If we failed tomorrow, then it would be over for us, and it would be all my fault. I would be sacrificed, and the others would be burned at the stake for being heretics.

"Don't worry about me," Nikki said. "We're going to get out of here and everything's going to be okay." She placed her hand on my cheek and gave me a small smile. "Your mother would've wanted you to get out of here."

"My mother didn't know what she wanted," I said curtly. I turned over, moving Nikki's hand away from my face.

"Just remember the plan," she said. "We're with you all the way, but we need you all in." Which translated into they needed me to pull myself together. It was the only way we would get this done.

"Okay."

Nikki leaned towards me. I felt the softness of her lips against my ear as she whispered to me. "We only have one shot to get this right."

CHAPTER 35

"Can this day be over already?" I muttered to myself. Nikki nodded in agreement. She looked as if she was about to vomit.

Even though I spoke quietly, my voice seemed to echo across the lawn as we ate lunch. Some people turned around to look at me. Others continued to stare down into their mush. Genevieve was one of the few who had turned to look at me. She had fear in her eyes.

The day dragged on. When it was finally time to go to the church, Brayley asked to visit my mother's grave one last time. I agreed, and we found one white rose before heading over to the cemetery.

While standing over my mother's grave, I did something that I hadn't done in a long time. I prayed. I prayed for our plan to work.

Once we were done, Brayley held my hand as we walked to the church. His hands were sweaty, and he looked as if he was about to faint.

"Are you sure we can do this?" Brayley whispered. The closer we got to the forming crowd, the more my stomach twisted and turned.

"We'll be fine," I whispered to him as we took our places in the back of the crowd.

He looked up at me and gave me a small smile, but I could tell that he wasn't reassured. Once everyone had been gathered, the bell rang signaling the start of the Annual Harvest.

Every year we were forced to watch this horrific act carried out. Every year we were forced to partake in this ceremony. Josef always said it was something we had to do. That it was how we pleased our God, but now that I knew the truth of why we were doing this, it terrified me. We weren't pleasing God. We were pleasing a witch.

The bell stopped, and Josef cleared his throat. "Good afternoon Blue Corn."

"Good afternoon," the crowd answered back.

"We are here today to celebrate our Annual Harvest," Josef said. "The final one."

I looked down at the ground. I couldn't stand to look at him. I was sickened.

"The Annual Harvest started in 1915. The year that this community was born. My great-great grandfather created Blue Corn as a haven to rid ourselves of worldly wrongs and to become one with our heavenly father. For one hundred years, we have been examples of what this world should be like," Josef smiled. "But with great success comes a great price. The Annual Harvest is that great price. There is no bad without the good, and there is no good without the bad. For that, we must pay for our continued nourishment in the form of a sacrifice." Josef's eyes moved over the crowd.

"One," he continued, holding his index finger up. "One sacrifice must be made to pay our debts. To restore order. To keep us alive. Although today feels like a day of mourning, it is meant to be a day of celebration. Everyone should be rejoicing because we are paying our dues. We are pleasing our God as instruments of his mercy." Some people in the crowd nodded in agreement. "Let us pray."

We all got down on our knees. Everyone bowed their heads. I stared down at the ground, waiting.

"Lord, I ask for guidance. I know you will lead me to the right name and I thank them for being willing to sacrifice for the greater good. Amen."

"Amen," the crowd repeated.

We all looked up and watched as Danny walked up to Josef holding a glass bowl in his hands. Danny caught my eye and nodded. I held my breath as Josef dug into the bowl. He pulled out a strip of paper and read the name aloud.

"Brayley Harbuck."

There was a collective sigh as the crowd murmured their thanks. I was expecting to hear Brayley's name yet I was still shocked. I finally came to when I felt Brayley's hand tighten in mine. I had positioned us near the back of the crowd for a reason, and it had paid off. I was able to pull Brayley away from them just as they reached their hands to grab him. Josef's voice yelled over the crowd to grab the both of us. I started to run, but I stopped as my arm was yanked. I looked back to see that an older woman had grabbed Brayley.

"Let him go!" I yelled, pulling him to me.

"October, help!" Brayley yelled as the woman tightened her grip on his wrist.

"Let him go!" I yelled, yanking his arm as hard as I could. He broke free from the woman's grasp. "Run!"

We ran as fast as we could towards the cornfields. I could hear the crowd behind us. I imagined that Brayley and I must've looked like maniacs, but the rush was exhilarating.

Brayley and I finally reached the cornfields and stopped once we had gotten a little further in. We could still hear them. Their shouts and screams sounded furious. My blood raced in my ear, and my chest heaved up and down from running.

"You're okay?" I asked him.

"Yeah," he said breathlessly.

On my right, the leaves rustled and familiar faces came out of the stalks. I heaved a sigh of relief and ran into Drew's arms. I knew we had to leave, but being in his arms comforted me for just a moment. I looked over Drew's shoulder to see that Ward, Nikki, and Zan stood behind him. They all looked out of breath from running.

"Where's Father?" I asked Ward.

"He's coming," Ward said, stepping towards us. "But we have to go."

I shook my head. "No. I'm not leaving without him."

"They're gonna find us," Ward said. "We can't stay."

Suddenly, a gunshot rocked the air. It sounded close.

"We have to go!" Drew yelled.

I grabbed Brayley's hand and gave it to Drew. "Take him," I said. "I'll meet you."

"October-"

"Please," I said. "I won't be long."

Drew nodded and grabbed Brayley's hand. "You promise?'

I did and pulled Drew close to me so that our lips touched. We kissed, and for a second I didn't feel so in danger. I pulled away from him. "Go."

He took Brayley's hand and ran. Nikki and Zan followed behind them. I looked at Ward.

"You're coming with me?" Ward nodded and pulled out a gun from behind his back. "You have one too."

"Yes," Ward said. "Now stay close."

I nodded and followed behind him as we ran in the direction of the woods. Just as we reached the edge of the cornfields, another gunshot went off making me fall to the ground taking Ward with me. I could hear a man screaming in pain. It sounded like my father.

"No!" I yelled. Ward held onto me as I tried to fight against him.

"They'll find us, October, and Josef will kill us. We have to go!"

"No!" I yelled. "I'm not leaving without our father!" I got up, and Ward tried to stop me, but he wasn't quick enough. As I exited the cornfields, I saw my father lying on the ground near the edge of the woods. I ran to him to see him clutching his bloody shoulder gasping for air. I knelt beside him.

"How bad is it?" I asked.

"Bad," he managed to get out.

Above us the clouds dropped. The rain came down hard and fast. I looked behind me to see Ward running towards us.

"We have to help him," I yelled over the roar of the wind.

Instead of arguing with me, he answered. "Okay."

I could feel the weight of my father as we lifted him off the ground. One of his arms wrapped around my neck and the other wrapped around Ward. Watery wind blew over my body, making my hair stick to my face. The wind and rain was loud, but I could still hear my father's voice in my ear. "Thank you."

"I'm getting us out of here," I said to him.

To be almost free was a giddy feeling. I felt tingly all over my body, but I wasn't certain that we were going to make it. I was about to do the impossible. Blue Corn would finally be a thing of the past.

I didn't dare turn around to see who was following us. I was afraid that I would see Josef. That his hands would be outstretched ready to yank us back inside.

But no one stopped us. Our steps and my father's ragged breathing was all the sound I could hear. Finally, my father's breathing slowed. It was like the water was strengthening him. I could feel him growing stronger as the rain slowed ever slightly. It was as if his body was synced to the rain in some way. The rain suddenly made me think of the day when my mother came out of her grief.

It was after we had gotten home from evening worship, and I remember finding my mother standing outside in the rain. She had her head held back and her mouth wide open as it filled with rain water. She had looked back at me, and that was when she had beckoned me to come to her. I held her hand, and we stood together in the rain.

"It's gonna be alright, October," she had said. She looked at me, and her eyes were an electric blue. "It's gonna be alright."

My mother was finally happy that day. I didn't know why. It was as if the rain had brought her back to life.

We continued to drag our father towards the fence. His shoulder was still bleeding, but his breathing was back to normal. He looked at me with a small smile. I smiled back.

"We're almost there," Ward said.

"Good," my father said.

When we finally got to the fence, I didn't see the others at first. It was my father's voice that guided me in their direction.

"What's wrong?" my father asked.

I looked over to see the others huddled around something on the ground. Drew was hunched over a small body as Nikki sobbed madly. Zan lay a few feet away from them.

"What's going on?" I asked.

No one answered. I pulled away from my father and ran towards them. As I got closer, I stumbled and fell to the ground. I tried to get up, but the slippery ground was holding me back.

"October, no!" Drew yelled for me to stay back.

"Is that him?" I asked. I crawled towards them like a blind woman groping her way along. I screamed.

Drew was hunched over Brayley's lifeless body. Blood covered his shirt and around his neck. He had been stabbed in the chest. His blank eyes stared up into the air.

"What happened?" I could hear Ward ask.

"It was Zan," Nikki said. She was hysterical. Her words were shaky. "He turned on us. He had a knife. October, I'm so sorry..."

I couldn't hear what she said after that. I could only hear my screams. I pressed my forehead to Brayley's chest. I was hoping to feel a heartbeat. I wanted to feel the rise and fall of his chest, but I felt nothing. My father knelt beside me and picked Brayley up. He held him against him as he sobbed in the crook of my brother's neck.

"We have to go now," Ward pleaded. "Or we're not going to make it."

The sound of another gunshot startled all of us. Someone wrapped their hands around my waist and pulled me off of the ground.

"October!" Drew held me. I kicked and yelled in his arms. "October! Please!"

I stopped. I rested my head against Drew's solid chest and breathed. My heart pounded against my chest, and my breath came out in short huffs.

"We have to go, October," Drew whispered to me.

I closed my eyes, but I couldn't shake the image of Brayley's dead body. The only satisfaction that I would have was knowing that my mother would be there to greet him.

We started to run. The adrenaline must have clouded my mind because I felt like I was flying as we raced to the fence's entrance. I could barely feel Drew's grip on my arm as he pulled me along.

My mother and brother were dead. My father was alive, and I was going to have a new life. My brother would have asked that I return to Blue Corn one day to help anyone else who wanted to escape. He was as close to an angel on Earth than I would ever be.

But he was still now. And I would never go back.

ACKNOWLEDGEMENTS

I have kept this book a secret to so many of my friends and family, but the few that I have told have been encouraging and I thank you. This book has been a long time coming and for five years it has changed many times. I'm glad to finally have a final piece to share.

To my family and friends, thank you for understanding when I am deep in "writer's mode."

Thank you to Crystal for being my first beta reader. You liking the sample that I sent to you gave me the hope that others will enjoy it as well. I would also like to thank my inspiration, author Stephen King. Without you, horror fiction wouldn't be where it is today. I have been in love with horror ever since I was a small child and I will always be a proud horror junkie.

Finally, I would like to thank my mother. You were my first reader and your love and encouragement of my writing will always be appreciated. If no one else reads my book, I can always count on you. Thank you.

ABOUT THE AUTHOR

Charity Williams grew up in Americus, Georgia, a small town. She attended Georgia Southern University Armstrong Campus (formerly Armstrong State University). She received her BA in English and a minor in Writing. She has always been interested in telling stories from a very young age and decided to write her first full length novel in 2015.

FROM THE AUTHOR

Readers…

Thank you for reading *October's Harvest*. I hope you enjoyed this novel. If you have a moment, please review *October's Harvest* at the store where you bought it. I read and appreciate each and every one of them. They help motivate me to keep writing and motivate me to write a better book!

Made in the USA
Middletown, DE
28 October 2023

41508287R00163